Death in Ve

Thomas Mann

(Translator: Kenneth Burke)

Alpha Editions

This edition published in 2024

ISBN : 9789368393733

Design and Setting By
Alpha Editions
www.alphaedis.com
Email - info@alphaedis.com

As per information held with us this book is in Public Domain.
This book is a reproduction of an important historical work. Alpha Editions uses the best technology to reproduce historical work in the same manner it was first published to preserve its original nature. Any marks or number seen are left intentionally to preserve its true form.

I

On a spring afternoon of the year 19—, when our continent lay under such threatening weather for whole months, Gustav Aschenbach, or von Aschenbach as his name read officially after his fiftieth birthday, had left his apartment on the Prinzregentenstrasse in Munich and had gone for a long walk. Overwrought by the trying and precarious work of the forenoon—which had demanded a maximum wariness, prudence, penetration, and rigour of the will—the writer had not been able even after the noon meal to break the impetus of the productive mechanism within him, that *motus animi continuus* which constitutes, according to Cicero, the foundation of eloquence; and he had not attained the healing sleep which—what with the increasing exhaustion of his strength—he needed in the middle of each day. So he had gone outdoors soon after tea, in the hopes that air and movement would restore him and prepare him for a profitable evening.

It was the beginning of May, and after cold, damp weeks a false midsummer had set in. The English Gardens, although the foliage was still fresh and sparse, were as pungent as in August, and in the parts nearer the city had been full of conveyances and promenaders. At the Aumeister, which he had reached by quieter and quieter paths, Aschenbach had surveyed for a short time the Wirtsgarten with its lively crowds and its border of cabs and carriages. From here, as the sun was sinking, he had started home, outside the park, across the open fields; and since he felt tired and a storm was threatening from the direction of Föhring, he waited at the North Cemetery for the tram which would take him directly back to the city.

It happened that he found no one in the station or its vicinity. There was not a vehicle to be seen, either on the paved Ungererstrasse, with its solitary glistening rails stretching out towards Schwabing, or on the Föhringer Chaussee. Behind the fences of the stone-masons' establishments, where the crosses, memorial tablets, and monuments standing for sale formed a second, uninhabited burial ground, there was no sign of life; and opposite him the Byzantine structure of the Funeral Hall lay silent in the reflection of the departing day; its façade, ornamented in luminous colours with Greek crosses and hieratic paintings, above which were displayed inscriptions symmetrically arranged in gold letters, and texts chosen to bear on the life beyond; such as, "They enter into the dwelling of the Lord," or, "The light of eternity shall shine upon them." And for some time as he stood waiting he found a grave diversion in spelling out the formulas and letting his mind's eye lose itself in their transparent mysticism, when, returning from his reveries, he noticed in the portico, above the two apocalyptic animals guarding the steps, a man whose somewhat unusual appearance gave his thoughts an entirely new direction.

Whether he had just now come out from the inside through the bronze door, or had approached and mounted from the outside unobserved, remained uncertain. Aschenbach, without applying himself especially to the matter, was inclined to believe the former. Of medium height, thin, smooth-shaven, and noticeably pug-nosed, the man belonged to the red-haired type and possessed the appropriate fresh milky complexion. Obviously, he was not of Bavarian extraction, since at least the white and straight-brimmed straw hat that covered his head gave his appearance the stamp of a foreigner, of someone who had come from a long distance. To be sure, he was wearing the customary knapsack strapped across his shoulders, and a belted suit of rough yellow wool; his left arm was resting on his thigh, and his grey storm cape was thrown across it. In his right hand he held a cane with an iron ferrule, which he had stuck diagonally into the ground, and, with his feet crossed, was leaning his hip against the crook. His head was raised so that the Adam's-apple protruded hard and bare on a scrawny neck emerging from a loose sport-shirt. And he was staring sharply off into the distance, with colourless, red-lidded eyes between which stood two strong, vertical wrinkles peculiarly suited to his short, turned-up nose. Thus—and perhaps his elevated position helped to give the impression—his bearing had something majestic and commanding about it, something bold, or even savage. For whether he was grimacing because he was blinded by the setting sun, or whether it was a case of a permanent distortion of the physiognomy, his lips seemed too short, they were so completely pulled back from his teeth that these were exposed even to the gums, and stood out white and long.

It is quite possible that Aschenbach, in his half-distracted, half-inquisitive examination of the stranger, had been somewhat inconsiderate, for he suddenly became aware that his look was being answered, and indeed so militantly, so straight in the eye, so plainly with the intention of driving the thing through to the very end and compelling him to capitulate, that he turned away uncomfortably and began walking along by the fences, deciding casually that he would pay no further attention to the man. The next minute he had forgotten him. But perhaps the exotic element in the stranger's appearance had worked on his imagination; or a new physical or spiritual influence of some sort had come into play. He was quite astonished to note a peculiar inner expansion, a kind of roving unrest, a youthful longing after far-off places: a feeling so vivid, so new, or so long dormant and neglected, that, with his hands behind his back and his eyes on the ground, he came to a sudden stop, and examined into the nature and purport of this emotion.

It was the desire for travel, nothing more; although, to be sure, it had attacked him violently, and was heightened to a passion, even to the point of an hallucination. His yearnings crystallized; his imagination, still in ferment from his hours of work, actually pictured all the marvels and terrors of a manifold world which it was suddenly struggling to conceive. He saw a landscape, a tropical swampland under a heavy, murky sky, damp, luxuriant, and enormous, a kind of prehistoric wilderness of islands, bogs, and arms of water, sluggish with mud; he saw, near him and in the distance, the hairy shafts of palms rising out of a rank lecherous thicket, out of places where the plant-life was fat, swollen, and blossoming exorbitantly; he saw strangely misshapen trees sending their roots into the ground, into stagnant pools with greenish reflections; and here, between floating flowers which were milk-white and large as dishes, birds of a strange nature, high-shouldered, with crooked bills, were standing in the muck, and looking motionlessly to one side; between dense, knotted stalks of bamboo he saw the glint from the eyes of a crouching tiger—and he felt his heart knocking with fear and with puzzling desires. Then the image disappeared; and with a shake of his head Aschenbach resumed his walk along past the fences of the stone-masons' establishments.

Since the time, at least, when he could command the means to enjoy the advantages of moving about the world as he pleased, he had considered travelling simply as an hygienic precaution which must be complied with now and then despite one's feelings and one's preferences. Too busy with the tasks arranged for him by his interest in his own ego and in the problems of Europe, too burdened with the onus of production, too little prone to diversion, and in no sense an amateur of the varied amusements of the great world, he had been thoroughly satisfied with such knowledge of the earth's surface as any one can get without moving far out of his own circle; and he had never even been tempted to leave Europe. Especially now that his life was slowly on the decline, and that the artist's fear of not having finished—this uneasiness lest the clock run down before he had done his part and given himself completely—could no longer be waived aside as a mere whim, he had confined his outer existence almost exclusively to the beautiful city which had become his home and to the rough country house which he had built in the mountains and where he spent the rainy summers.

Further, this thing which had laid hold of him so belatedly, but with such suddenness, was very readily moderated and adjusted by the force of his reason and of a discipline which he had practised since youth. He had intended carrying his life work forward to a certain point before removing to the country. And the thought of knocking about the world for months and neglecting his work during this time, seemed much too lax and contrary to his plans; it really could not be considered seriously. Yet he knew only too well what the reasons were for this unexpected temptation. It was the urge to escape—he admitted to himself—this yearning for the new and the remote, this appetite for freedom, for unburdening, for forgetfulness; it was a pressure away from his work, from the steady drudgery of a coldly passionate service. To be sure, he loved this work and almost loved the enervating battle that was fought daily between a proud tenacious will—so often tested—and this growing weariness which no one was to suspect and which must not betray itself in his productions by any sign of weakness or negligence. But it seemed wise not to draw the bow overtightly, and not to strangle by sheer obstinacy so strongly persistent an appetite. He thought of his work, thought of the place at which yesterday and now again to-day he had been forced to leave off, and which, it seemed, would yield neither to patience and coaxing nor to a definite attack. He examined it again, trying to break through or to circumvent the deadlock, but he gave up with a shudder of repugnance. There was no unusual difficulty here; what balked him were the scruples of aversion, which took the form of a fastidious insatiability. Even as a young man this insatiability had meant to him the very nature, the fullest essence, of talent; and for that reason he had restrained and chilled his emotions, since he was aware that they incline to content themselves with a happy approximation, a state of semi-completion. Were these enslaved emotions now taking their vengeance on him, by leaving him in the lurch, by refusing to forward and lubricate his art; and were they bearing off with them every enjoyment, every live interest in form and expression?

Not that he was producing anything bad; his years gave him at least this advantage, that he felt himself at all times in full and easy possession of his craftsmanship. But while the nation honoured him for this, he himself was not content; and it seemed to him that his work lacked the marks of that fiery and fluctuating emotionalism which is an enormous thing in one's favour, and which, while it argues an enjoyment on the part of the author, also constitutes, more than any depth of content, the enjoyment of the amateur. He feared the summer in the country, alone in the little house with the maid who prepared his meals, and the servant who brought them to him. He feared the familiar view of the mountain peaks and the slopes which would stand about him in his boredom and his discontent. Consequently there was need of a break in some new direction. If the summer was to be endurable and productive, he must attempt something out of his usual orbit; he must relax, get a change of air, bring an element of freshness into the blood. To travel, then—that much was settled. Not far, not all the way to the tigers. But one night on the sleeper, and a rest of three or four weeks at some pleasant popular resort in the South....

He thought this out while the noise of the electric tram came nearer along the Ungererstrasse; and as he boarded it he decided to devote the evening to the study of maps and time-tables. On the platform it occurred to him to look around for the man in the straw hat, his companion during that most significant time spent waiting at the station. But his whereabouts remained uncertain, as he was not to be seen either at the place where he was formerly standing, or anywhere else in the vicinity of the station, or on the car itself.

II

The author of that lucid and powerful prose epic built around the life of Frederick of Prussia; the tenacious artist who, after long application, wove rich, varied strands of human destiny together under one single predominating theme in the fictional tapestry known as Maya; the creator of that stark tale which is called The Wretch and which pointed out for an entire oncoming generation the possibility of some moral certainty beyond pure knowledge; finally, the writer (and this sums up briefly the works of his mature period) of the impassioned treatise on Art and the Spirit, whose capacity for mustering facts, and, further, whose fluency in their presentation, led cautious judges to place this treatise alongside Schiller's conclusions on naïve and sentimental poetry—Gustav Aschenbach, then, was the son of a higher law official, and was born in L——, a leading city in the Province of Silesia. His forbears had been officers, magistrates, government functionaries, men who had led severe, steady lives serving their king, their state. A deeper strain of spirituality had been manifest in them once, in the person of a preacher; the preceding generation had brought a brisker, more sensuous blood into the family through the author's mother, daughter of a Bohemian band-master. The traces of foreignness in his features came from her. A marriage of sober painstaking conscientiousness with impulses of a darker, more fiery nature had had an artist as its result, and this particular artist.

Since his whole nature was centred around acquiring a reputation, he showed himself, if not exactly precocious, at least (thanks to the firmness and pithiness of his personality, his accent) ripened and adjusted to the public at an early age. Almost as a schoolboy he had made a name for himself. Within ten years he had learned to face the world through the medium of his writing-table, to discharge the obligations of his fame in a correspondence which (since many claims are pressed on the successful, the trustworthy) had to be brief as well as pleasant and to the point. At forty, wearied by the vicissitudes and the exertion of his own work, he had to manage a daily mail which bore the postmarks of countries in all parts of the world.

Equally removed from the banal and the eccentric, his talents were so constituted as to gain both the confidence of the general public and the stable admiration and sympathy of the critical. Thus even as a young man continually devoted to the pursuit of craftsmanship—and that of no ordinary kind—he had never known the careless freedom of youth. When, around thirty-five years of age, he had been taken ill in Vienna, one sharp observer said of him in company, "You see, Aschenbach has always lived like this," and the speaker contracted the fingers of his left hand into a fist; "never like this," and he let his open hand droop comfortably from the arm of his chair.

That hit the mark; and the heroic, the ethical about it all was that he was not of a strong constitution, and though he was pledged by his nature to these steady efforts, he was not really born to them.

Considerations of ill-health had kept him from attending school as a boy, and had compelled him to receive instruction at home. He had grown up alone, without comrades—and he was forced to realize soon enough that he belonged to a race which often lacked, not talent, but that physical substructure which talent relies on for its fullest fruition: a race accustomed to giving its best early, and seldom extending its faculties over the years. But his favourite phrase was "carrying through"; in his novel on Frederick he saw the pure apotheosis of this command, which struck him as the essential concept of the virtuous in action and passion. Also, he wished earnestly to grow old, since he had always maintained that the only artistry which can be called truly great, comprehensive, yes even truly admirable, is that which is permitted to bear fruits characteristic of each stage in human development.

Since he must carry the responsibilities of his talent on frail shoulders, and wanted to go a long way, the primary requirement was discipline—and fortunately discipline was his direct inheritance from his father's side. By forty, fifty, or at an earlier age when others are still slashing about with enthusiasm, and are contentedly putting off to some later date the execution of plans on a large scale, he would start the day early, dashing cold water over his chest and back, and then with a couple of tall wax candles in silver candlesticks at the head of his manuscript, he would pay out to his art, in two or three eager, scrupulous morning hours, the strength which he had accumulated in sleep. It was pardonable, indeed it was a direct tribute to the effectiveness of his moral scheme, that the uninitiated took his Maya world, and the massive epic machinery upon which the life of the hero Frederick was unrolled, as evidence of long breath and sustaining power. While actually they had been built up layer by layer, in small daily allotments, through hundreds and hundreds of single inspirations. And if they were so excellent in both composition and texture, it was solely because their creator had held out for years under the strain of one single work, with a steadiness of will and a tenacity comparable to that which conquered his native province; and because, finally, he had turned over his most vital and valuable hours to the problem of minute revision.

In order that a significant work of the mind may exert immediately some broad and deep effect, a secret relationship, or even conformity, must exist between the personal destiny of the author and the common destiny of his contemporaries. People do not know why they raise a work of art to fame. Far from being connoisseurs, they believe that they see in it hundreds of virtues which justify so much interest; but the true reason for their applause is an unconscious sympathy. Aschenbach had once stated quite plainly in some remote place that nearly everything great which comes into being does so in spite of something—in spite of sorrow or suffering, poverty, destitution, physical weakness, depravity, passion, or a thousand other handicaps. But that was not merely an observation; it was a discovery, the formula of his life and reputation, the key to his work. And what wonder then that it was also the distinguishing moral trait, the dominating gesture, of his most characteristic figures?

Years before, one shrewd analyst had written of the new hero-type to which this author gave preference, and which kept turning up in variations of one sort or another: he called it the conception of "an intellectual and youthful masculinity" which "stands motionless, haughty, ashamed, with jaw set, while swords and spear-points beset the body." That was beautiful and ingenious; and it was exact, although it may have seemed to suggest too much passivity. For to be poised against fatality, to meet adverse conditions gracefully, is more than simple endurance; it is an act of aggression, a positive triumph—and the figure of Sebastian is the most beautiful figure, if not of art as a whole, at least of the art of literature. Looking into this fictional world, one saw: a delicate self-mastery by which any inner deterioration, any biological decay was kept concealed from the eyes of the world; a crude, vicious sensuality capable of fanning its rising passions into pure flame, yes, even of mounting to dominance in the realm of beauty; a pallid weakness which draws from the glowing depths of the soul the strength to bow whole arrogant peoples before the foot of the cross, or before the feet of weakness itself; a charming manner maintained in his cold, strict service to form; a false, precarious mode of living, and the keenly enervating melancholy and artifice of the born deceiver—to observe such trials as this was enough to make one question whether there really was any heroism other than weakness. And in any case, what heroism could be more in keeping with the times? Gustav Aschenbach was the one poet among the many workers on the verge of exhaustion: all those over-burdened, used-up, tenacious moralists of production who, delicately built and destitute of means, can rely for a time at least on will-power and the shrewd husbandry of their resources to secure the effects of greatness. There are many such: they are the heroes of the period. And they all found themselves in his works; here they were indeed, upheld, intensified, applauded; they were grateful to him, they acclaimed him.

In his time he had been young and raw; and misled by his age he had blundered in public. He had stumbled, had exposed himself; both in writing and in talk he had offended against caution and tact. But he had acquired the dignity which, as he insisted, is the innate goad and craving of every great talent; in fact, it could be said that his entire development had been a conscious undeviating progression away from the embarrassments of scepticism and irony, and towards dignity.

The general masses are satisfied by vigour and tangibility of treatment rather than by any close intellectual processes; but youth, with its passion for the absolute, can be arrested only by the problematical. And Aschenbach had been absolute, problematical, as only a youth could be. He had been a slave to the intellect, had played havoc with knowledge, had ground up his seed crops, had divulged secrets, had discredited talent, had betrayed art—yes, while his modellings were entertaining the faithful votaries, filling them with enthusiasm, making their lives more keen, this youthful artist was taking the breath away from the generation then in its twenties by his cynicisms on the questionable nature of art, and of artistry itself.

But it seems that nothing blunts the edge of a noble, robust mind more quickly and more thoroughly than the sharp and bitter corrosion of knowledge; and certainly the moody radicalism of the youth, no matter how conscientious, was shallow in comparison with his firm determination as an older man and a master to deny knowledge, to reject it, to pass it with raised head, in so far as it is capable of crippling, discouraging, or degrading to the slightest degree, our will, acts, feelings, or even passions. How else could the famous story of The Wretch be understood than as an outburst of repugnance against the disreputable psychologism of the times: embodied in the figure of that soft and stupid half-clown who pilfers a destiny for himself by guiding his wife (from powerlessness, from lasciviousness, from ethical frailty) into the arms of an adolescent, and believes that he may through profundity commit vileness? The verbal pressure with which he here cast out the outcast announced the return from every moral scepticism, from all fellow-feeling with the engulfed: it was the counter-move to the laxity of the sympathetic principle that to understand all is to forgive all—and the thing that was here well begun, even nearly completed, was that "miracle of reborn ingenuousness" which was taken up a little later in one of the author's dialogues expressly and not without a certain discreet emphasis. Strange coincidences! Was it as a result of this rebirth, this new dignity and sternness, that his feeling for beauty—a discriminating purity, simplicity, and evenness of attack which henceforth gave his productions such an obvious, even such a deliberate stamp of mastery and classicism—showed an almost excessive strengthening about this time? But ethical resoluteness in the exclusion of science, of emancipatory and restrictive knowledge—does this not in turn signify a simplification, a reduction morally of the world to too limited terms, and thus also a strengthened capacity for the forbidden, the evil, the morally impossible? And does not form have two aspects? Is it not moral and unmoral at once—moral in that it is the result and expression of discipline, but unmoral, and even immoral, in that by nature it contains an indifference to morality, is calculated, in fact, to make morality bend beneath its proud and unencumbered sceptre?

Be that as it may. An evolution is a destiny; and why should his evolution, which had been upheld by the general confidence of a vast public, not run through a different course from one accomplished outside the lustre and the entanglements of fame? Only chronic vagabondage will find it tedious and be inclined to scoff when a great talent outgrows the libertine chrysalis-stage, learns to seize upon and express the dignity of the mind, and superimposes a formal etiquette upon a solitude which had been filled with unchastened and rigidly isolated sufferings and struggles and had brought all this to a point of power and honour among men. Further, how much sport, defiance, indulgence there is in the self-formation of a talent! Gradually something official, didactic crept into Gustav Aschenbach's productions, his style in later life fought shy of any abruptness and boldness, any subtle and unexpected contrasts; he inclined towards the fixed and standardized, the conventionally elegant, the conservative, the formal, the formulated, nearly. And, as is traditionally said of Louis XIV, with the advancing years he came to omit every common word from his vocabulary. At about this time it happened that the educational authorities included selected pages by him in their prescribed school readers. This was deeply sympathetic to his nature, and he did not decline when a German prince who had just mounted to the throne raised the author of the Frederick to nobility on the occasion of his fiftieth birthday. After a few years of unrest, a few tentative stopping-places here and there, he soon chose Munich as his permanent home, and lived there in a state of middle-class respectability such as fits in with the life of the mind in certain individual instances. The marriage which, when still young, he had contracted with a girl of an educated family came to an end with her death after a short period of happiness. He was left with a daughter, now married. He had never had a son.

Gustav von Aschenbach was somewhat below average height, dark, and smooth-shaven. His head seemed a bit too large in comparison with his almost dapper figure. His hair was brushed straight back, thinning out towards the crown, but very full about the temples, and strongly marked with grey; it framed a high, ridged forehead. Gold spectacles with rimless lenses cut into the bridge of his bold, heavy nose. The mouth was big, sometimes drooping, sometimes suddenly pinched and firm. His cheeks were thin and wrinkled, his well-formed chin had a slight cleft. This head, usually bent patiently to one side, seemed to have gone through momentous experiences, and yet it was his art which had produced those effects in his face, effects which are elsewhere the result of hard and agitated living. Behind this brow the brilliant repartee of the dialogue on war between Voltaire and the king had been born; these eyes, peering steadily and wearily from behind their glasses, had seen the bloody inferno of the lazaret in the Seven Years' War. Even as it applies to the individual, art is a heightened mode of existence. It gives deeper pleasures, it consumes more quickly. It carves into its servants' faces the marks of imaginary and spiritual adventures, and though their external activities may be as quiet as a cloister, it produces a lasting voluptuousness, over-refinement, fatigue, and curiosity of the nerves such as can barely result from a life filled with illicit passions and enjoyments.

III

Various matters of a literary and social nature delayed his departure until about two weeks after that walk in Munich. Finally he gave orders to have his country house ready for occupancy within a month; and one day between the middle and the end of May he took the night train for Trieste, where he made a stop-over of only twenty-four hours, and embarked the following morning for Pola.

What he was hunting was something foreign and unrelated to himself which would at the same time be quickly within reach; and so he stopped at an island in the Adriatic which had become well-known in recent years. It lay not far off the Istrian coast, with beautifully rugged cliffs fronting the open sea, and natives who dressed in variegated tatters and made strange sounds when they spoke. But rain and a heavy atmosphere, a provincial and exclusively Austrian patronage at the hotel, and the lack of that restfully intimate association with the sea which can be gotten only by a soft, sandy beach, irritated him, and prevented him from feeling that he had found the place he was looking for. Something within was disturbing him, and drawing him he was not sure where. He studied sailing dates, he looked about him questioningly, and of a sudden, as a thing both astounding and self-evident, his goal was before him. If you wanted to reach over night the unique, the fabulously different, where did you go? But that was plain. What was he doing here? He had lost the trail. He had wanted to go there. He did not delay in giving notice of his mistake in stopping here. In the early morning mist, a week and a half after his arrival on the island, a fast motorboat was carrying him and his luggage back over the water to the naval port, and he landed there just long enough to cross the gangplank to the damp deck of a ship which was lying under steam ready for the voyage to Venice.

It was an old hulk flying the Italian flag, decrepit, sooty, and mournful. In a cave-like, artificially lighted inside cabin where Aschenbach, immediately upon boarding the ship, was conducted by a dirty hunchbacked sailor who smirked politely, there was sitting behind a table, his hat cocked over his forehead and a cigarette stump in the corner of his mouth, a man with a goatee, and with the face of an old-style circus director, who was taking down the particulars of the passengers with professional grimaces and distributing the tickets. "To Venice!" he repeated Aschenbach's request, as he extended his arm and plunged his pen into the pasty dregs of a precariously tilted inkwell. "To Venice, first class! At your service, sir." And he wrote a generous scrawl, sprinkled it with blue sand out of a box, let the sand run off into a clay bowl, folded the paper with sallow, bony fingers, and began writing again. "A happily chosen destination!" he chatted on. "Ah, Venice! A splendid city! A city of irresistible attractiveness for the educated on account of its history as well as its present-day charms!" The smooth rapidity of his movements and the empty words accompanying them had something anaesthetic and reassuring about them, much as though he feared lest the traveller might still be vacillating in his decision to go to Venice. He handled the cash briskly, and let the change fall on the spotted table-cover with the skill of a croupier. "A pleasant journey, sir!" he said with a theatrical bow. "Gentlemen, I have the honour of serving you!" he called out immediately after, with his arm upraised, and he acted as if business were in full swing, although no one else was there to require his attention. Aschenbach returned to the deck.

With one arm on the railing, he watched the passengers on board and the idlers who loitered around the dock waiting for the ship to sail. The second class passengers, men and women, were huddled together on the foredeck, using boxes and bundles as seats. A group of young people made up the travellers on the first deck, clerks from Pola, it seemed, who had gathered in the greatest excitement for an excursion to Italy. They made a considerable fuss about themselves and their enterprise, chattered, laughed, enjoyed their own antics self-contentedly, and, leaning over the hand-rails, shouted flippantly and mockingly at their comrades who, with portfolios under their arms, were going up and down the waterfront on business and kept threatening the picnickers with their canes. One, in a bright yellow summer suit of ultra-fashionable cut, with a red necktie, and a rakishly tilted panama, surpassed all the others in his crowing good humour. But as soon as Aschenbach looked at him a bit more carefully, he discovered with a kind of horror that the youth was a cheat. He was old, that was unquestionable. There were wrinkles around his eyes and mouth. The faint crimson of the cheeks was paint, the hair under his brilliantly decorated straw hat was a wig; his neck was hollow and stringy, his turned-up moustache and the imperial on his chin were dyed; the full set of yellow teeth which he displayed when he laughed, a cheap artificial plate; and his hands, with signet rings on both index fingers, were those of an old man. Fascinated with loathing, Aschenbach watched him in his intercourse with his friends. Did they not know, did they not observe that he was old, that he was not entitled to wear their bright, foppish clothing, that he was not entitled to play at being one of them? Unquestioningly, and as quite the usual thing, it seemed, they allowed him among them, treating him as one of their own kind and returning his jovial nudges in the ribs without repugnance. How could that be? Aschenbach laid his hand on his forehead and closed his eyes; they were hot, since he had had too little sleep. He felt as though everything were not quite the same as usual, as though some dream-like estrangement, some peculiar distortion of the world, were beginning to take possession of him, and perhaps this could be stopped if he hid his face for a time and then looked around him again. Yet at this moment he felt as though he were swimming;

and looking up with an unreasoned fear, he discovered that the heavy, lugubrious body of the ship was separating slowly from the walled bank. Inch by inch, with the driving and reversing of the engine, the strip of dirty glistening water widened between the dock and the side of the ship; and after cumbersome manoeuvring, the steamer finally turned its nose towards the open sea. Aschenbach crossed to the starboard side, where the hunchback had set up a deck-chair for him, and a steward in a spotted dress-coat asked after his wants.

The sky was grey, the wind damp. Harbour and islands had been left behind, and soon all land was lost in the haze. Flakes of coal dust, bloated with moisture, fell over the washed deck, which would not dry. After the first hour an awning was spread, since it had begun to rain.

Bundled up in his coat, a book in his lap, the traveller rested, and the hours passed unnoticed. It stopped raining; the canvas awning was removed. The horizon was unbroken. The sea, empty, like an enormous disk, lay stretched under the curve of the sky. But in empty inarticulate space our senses lose also the dimensions of time, and we slip into the incommensurate. As he rested, strange shadowy figures, the old dandy, the goatee from the inside cabin, passed through his mind, with vague gestures, muddled dream-words—and he was asleep.

About noon he was called to a meal down in the corridor-like dining-hall into which the doors opened from the sleeping-cabins; he ate near the head of a long table, at the other end of which the clerks including the old man had been drinking with the boisterous captain since ten o'clock. The food was poor, and he finished rapidly. He felt driven outside to look at the sky, to see if it showed signs of being brighter above Venice.

He had kept thinking that this had to occur, since the city had always received him in full blaze. But sky and sea remained dreary and leaden, at times a misty rain fell, and here he was reaching by water a different Venice than he had ever found when approaching on land. He stood by the forestays, looking in the distance, waiting for land. He thought of the heavy-hearted, enthusiastic poet for whom the domes and bell towers of his dreams had once risen out of these waters; he relived in silence some of that reverence, happiness, and sorrow which had been turned then into cautious song; and easily susceptible to sensations already moulded, he asked himself wearily and earnestly whether some new enchantment and distraction, some belated adventure of the emotions, might still be held in store for this idle traveller.

Then the flat coast emerged on the right; the sea was alive with fishing smacks; the bathers' island appeared; it dropped behind to the left, the steamer slowly entered the narrow port which is named after it; and on the lagoon, facing gay ramshackle houses, it stopped completely, since it had to wait for the barque of the health department.

An hour passed before it appeared. He had arrived, and yet he had not; no one was in any hurry, no one was driven by impatience. The young men from Pola, patriotically attracted by the military bugle calls which rang over the water from the vicinity of the public gardens, had come on deck, and warmed by their Asti, they burst out with cheers for the drilling *bersagliere*. But it was repulsive to see what a state the primped-up old man had been brought to by his comradeship with youth. His old head was not able to resist its wine like the young and robust: he was painfully drunk. With glazed eyes, a cigarette between his trembling fingers, he stood in one place, swaying backwards and forwards from giddiness, and balancing himself laboriously. Since he would have fallen at the first step, he did not trust himself from the spot—yet he showed a deplorable insolence, buttonholed everyone who came near him, stammered, winked, and tittered, lifted his wrinkled, ornamented index finger in a stupid attempt at bantering, while he licked the corers of his mouth with his tongue in the most abominably suggestive manner. Aschenbach observed him darkly, and a feeling of numbness came over him again, as though the world were displaying a faint but irresistible tendency to distort itself into the peculiar and the grotesque: a feeling which circumstances prevented him from surrendering himself to completely, for just then the pounding activity of the engines commenced again, and the ship, resuming a voyage which had been interrupted so near its completion, passed through the San Marco canal.

So he saw it again, the most remarkable of landing places, that blinding composition of fantastic buildings which the Republic lays out before the eyes of approaching seafarers: the soft splendour of the palace, the Bridge of Sighs, on the bank the columns with lion and saint, the advancing, showy flank of the enchanted temple, the glimpse through to the archway, and the huge giant clock. And as he looked on he thought that to reach Venice by land, on the rail-road, was like entering a palace from the rear, and that the most unreal of cities should not be approached except as he was now doing, by ship, over the high seas.

The engine stopped, gondolas pressed in, the gangway was let down, customs officials climbed on board and discharged their duties perfunctorily; the disembarking could begin. Aschenbach made it understood that he wanted a gondola to take him and his luggage to the dock of those little steamers which ply between the city and the Lido, since he intended to locate near the sea. His plans were complied with, his wants were shouted down to the water, where the gondoliers were wrangling with one another in dialect. He was still hindered from descending; he was hindered by his trunk, which was being pulled and dragged with difficulty down the ladder-like steps. So that for some minutes he was not able to avoid the importunities of the atrocious old man, whose drunkenness gave him a sinister desire to do the foreigner parting honours. "We wish you a very agreeable visit," he bleated as he made an awkward bow. "We leave with pleasant recollections! *Au revoir, excusez*, and *bon jour*, your excellency!" His mouth watered, he pressed his eyes shut, he licked the corners of his mouth, and the dyed imperial turned up about his senile lips. "Our compliments," he mumbled, with two fingertips on his mouth, "our compliments to our sweetheart, the dearest prettiest sweetheart . . ." And suddenly his false upper teeth fell down on his lower lip. Aschenbach was able to escape. "To our sweetheart, our handsome sweetheart," he heard the cooing, hollow, stuttering voice behind him, while supporting himself against the handrail, he went down the gang-way.

Who would not have to suppress a fleeting shudder, a vague timidity and uneasiness, if it were a matter of boarding a Venetian gondola for the first time or after several years? The strange craft, an entirely unaltered survival from the times of balladry, with that peculiar blackness which is found elsewhere only in coffins—it suggests silent, criminal adventures in the rippling night, it suggests even more strongly death itself, the bier and the mournful funeral, and the last silent journey. And has it been observed that the seat of such a barque, this arm-chair of coffin-black veneer and dull black upholstery, is the softest, most luxuriant, most lulling seat in the world? Aschenbach noted this when he had relaxed at the feet of the gondolier, opposite his luggage, which lay neatly assembled on the prow. The rowers were still wrangling, harshly, incomprehensibly, with threatening gestures. But the strange silence of this canal city seemed to soften their voices, to disembody them, and dissipate them over the water. It was warm here in the harbour. Touched faintly by the warm breeze of the sirocco, leaning back against the limber portions of the cushions, the traveller closed his eyes in the enjoyment of a lassitude which was as unusual with him as it was sweet. The trip would be short, he thought; if only it went on for ever! He felt himself glide with a gentle motion away from the crowd and the confusion of voices.

It became quieter and quieter around him! There was nothing to be heard but the splashing of the oar, the hollow slapping of the waves against the prow of the boat as it stood above the water black and bold and armed with its halberd-like tip, and a third sound, of speaking, of whispering—the whispering of the gondolier, who was talking to himself between his teeth, fitfully, in words that were pressed out by the exertion of his arms. Aschenbach looked up, and was slightly astonished to discover that the lagoon was widening, and he was headed for the open sea. This seemed to indicate that he ought not to rest too much, but should see to it that his wishes were carried out.

"To the steamer dock!" he repeated, turning around completely and looking into the face of the gondolier who stood behind on a raised platform and towered up between him and the dun-coloured sky. He was a man of unpleasant, even brutal, appearance, dressed in sailor blue, with a yellow sash; a formless straw hat, its weave partially unravelled, was tilted insolently on his head. The set of his face, the blond curly moustache beneath a curtly turned-up nose, undoubtedly meant that he was not Italian. Although of somewhat frail build, so that one would not have thought him especially well suited to his trade, he handled the oar with great energy, throwing his entire body into each stroke. Occasionally, he drew back his lips from the exertion, and disclosed his white teeth. Wrinkling his reddish brows, he gazed on past his passenger, as he answered deliberately, almost gruffly: "You are going to the Lido." Aschenbach replied: "Of course. But I have just taken the gondola to get me across to San Marco. I want to use the *vaporetto*."

"You cannot use the *vaporetto*, sir."

"And why not?"

"Because the *vaporetto* will not haul luggage."

That was so; Aschenbach remembered. He was silent. But the fellow's harsh, presumptuous manner, so unusual towards a foreigner here, seemed unbearable. He said: "That is my affair. Perhaps I want to put my things in storage. You will turn back." There was silence. The oar splashed, the water thudded against the bow. And the talking and whispering began again. The gondolier was talking to himself between his teeth.

What was to be done? This man was strangely insolent, and had an uncanny decisiveness; the traveller, alone with him on the water, saw no way of getting what he wanted. And besides, how softly he could rest, if only he did not become excited! Hadn't he wanted the trip to go on and on for ever? It was wisest to let things take their course, and the main thing was that he was comfortable. The poison of inertia seemed to be issuing from the seat, from this low, black-upholstered arm-chair, so gently cradled by the oar strokes of the imperious gondolier behind him. The notion that he had fallen into the hands of a criminal passed dreamily across Aschenbach's mind—without the ability to summon his thoughts to an active defence. The possibility that it was all simply a plan for cheating him seemed more abhorrent. A feeling of duty or pride, a kind of recollection that one should prevent such things, gave him the strength to arouse himself once more. He asked: "What are you asking for the trip?"

Looking down upon him, the gondolier answered: "You will pay."

It was plain how this should be answered. Aschenbach said mechanically: "I shall pay nothing, absolutely nothing, if you don't take me where I want to go."

"You want to go to the Lido."

"But not with you."

"I am rowing you well."

That is so, Aschenbach thought, and relaxed. That is so; you are rowing me well. Even if you do have designs on my cash, and send me down to Pluto with a blow of your oar from behind, you will have rowed me well.

But nothing like that happened. They were even joined by others: a boatload of musical brigands, men and women, who sang to guitar and mandolin, riding persistently side by side with the gondola and filling the silence over the water with their covetous foreign poetry. A hat was held out, and Aschenbach threw in money. Then they stopped singing, and rowed away. And again the muttering of the gondolier could be heard as he talked fitfully and jerkily to himself.

So they arrived, tossed in the wake of a steamer plying towards the city. Two municipal officers, their hands behind their backs, their faces turned in the direction of the lagoon, were walking back and forth on the bank. Aschenbach left the gondola at the dock, supported by that old man who is stationed with his grappling hook at each one of Venice's landing-places. And since he had no small money, he crossed over to the hotel by the steamer wharf to get change and pay the rower what was due him. He got what he wanted in the lobby, he returned and found his travelling bags in a cart on the dock, and gondola and gondolier had vanished.

"He got out in a hurry," said the old man with the grappling hook. "A bad man, a man without a license, sir. He is the only gondolier who doesn't have a license. The others telephoned here."

Aschenbach shrugged his shoulders.

"The gentleman rode for nothing," the old man said, and held out his hat. Aschenbach tossed in a coin. He gave instructions to have his luggage taken to the beach hotel, and followed the cart through the avenue, the white-blossomed avenue which, lined on both sides with taverns, shops, and boarding houses, runs across the island to the shore.

He entered the spacious hotel from the rear, by the terraced garden, and passed through the vestibule and the lobby until he reached the desk. Since he had been announced, he was received with obliging promptness. A manager, a small frail flatteringly polite man with a black moustache and a

French style frock coat, accompanied him to the third floor in the lift, and showed him his room, an agreeable place furnished in cherry wood. It was decorated with strong-smelling flowers, and its high windows afforded a view out across the open sea. He stepped up to one of them after the employee had left; and while his luggage was being brought up and placed in the room behind him, he looked down on the beach (it was comparatively deserted in the afternoon) and on the sunless ocean which was at flood tide and was sending long low waves against the bank in a calm regular rhythm.

The experiences of a man who lives alone and in silence are both vaguer and more penetrating than those of people in society; his thoughts are heavier, more odd, and touched always with melancholy. Images and observations which could easily be disposed of by a glance, a smile, an exchange of opinion, will occupy him unbearably, sink deep into the silence, become full of meaning, become life, adventure, emotion. Loneliness ripens the eccentric, the daringly and estrangingly beautiful, the poetic. But loneliness also ripens the perverse, the disproportionate, the absurd, and the illicit.— So, the things he had met with on the trip, the ugly old fop with his twaddle about sweethearts, the lawbreaking gondolier who was cheated of his pay, still left the traveller uneasy. Without really providing any resistance to the mind, without offering any solid stuff to think over, they were nevertheless profoundly strange, as it seemed to him, and disturbing precisely because of this contradiction. In the meanwhile, he greeted the sea with his eyes, and felt pleasure at the knowledge that Venice was so conveniently near. Finally he turned away, bathed his face, left orders to the chambermaid for a few things he still needed done to make his comfort complete, and let himself be taken to the ground floor by the green-uniformed Swiss who operated the lift.

He took his tea on the terrace facing the ocean, then descended and followed the boardwalk for quite a way in the direction of the Hotel Excelsior. When he returned it seemed time to dress for dinner. He did this with his usual care and slowness, since he was accustomed to working over his toilette. And yet he came down a little early to the lobby where he found a great many of the hotel guests assembled, mixing distantly and with a show of mutual indifference to one another, but all waiting for meal time. He took a paper from the table, dropped into a leather chair, and observed the company; they differed agreeably from the guests where he had first stopped.

A wide and tolerantly inclusive horizon was spread out before him. Sounds of all the principal languages formed a subdued murmur. The accepted evening dress, a uniform of good manners, brought all human varieties into a fitting unity. There were Americans with their long wry features, large Russian families, English ladies, German children with French nurses. The Slavic element seemed to predominate. Polish was being spoken nearby.

It was a group of children gathered around a little wicker table, under the protection of a teacher or governess: three young girls, apparently fifteen to seventeen, and a long-haired boy about fourteen years old. With astonishment Aschenbach noted that the boy was absolutely beautiful. His face, pale and reserved, framed with honey-coloured hair, the straight sloping nose, the lovely mouth, the expression of sweet and godlike seriousness, recalled Greek sculpture of the noblest period; and the complete purity of the forms was accompanied by such a rare personal charm that, as he watched, he felt that he had never met with anything equally felicitous in nature or the plastic arts. He was further struck by the obviously intentional contrast with the principles of upbringing which showed in the sisters' attire and bearing. The three girls, the eldest of whom could be considered grown up, were dressed with a chasteness and severity bordering on disfigurement. Uniformly cloister-like costumes, of medium length, slate-coloured, sober, and deliberately unbecoming in cut, with white turned-down collars as the only relief, suppressed every possible appeal of shapeliness. Their hair, brushed down flat and tight against the head, gave their faces a nunlike emptiness and lack of character. Surely this was a mother's influence, and it had not even occurred to her to apply the pedagogical strictness to the boy which she seemed to find necessary for her girls. It was clear that in his existence the first factors were gentleness and tenderness. The shears had been resolutely kept from his beautiful hair; like a Prince Charming's, it fell in curls over his forehead, his ears, and still deeper, across his neck. The English sailor suit, with its braids, stitchings, and embroideries, its puffy sleeves narrowing at the ends and fitting snugly about the fine wrists of his still childish but slender hands, gave the delicate figure something rich and luxurious. He was sitting, half profile to the observer, one foot in its black patent-leather shoe placed before the other, an elbow resting on the arm of his wicker chair, a cheek pressed against his fist, in a position of negligent good manners, entirely free of the almost subservient stiffness to which his sisters seemed accustomed. Did he have some illness? For his skin stood out as white as ivory against the golden darkness of the surrounding curls. Or was he simply a pampered favourite child, made this way by a doting and moody love? Aschenbach inclined to believe the latter. Almost every artist is born with a rich and treacherous tendency to recognize injustices which have created beauty, and to meet aristocratic distinction with sympathy and reverence.

A waiter passed through and announced in English that the meal was ready. Gradually the guests disappeared through the glass door into the dining hall. Stragglers crossed, coming from the entrance, or the lifts. Inside, they had already begun serving, but the young Poles were still waiting around the little wicker table; and Aschenbach, comfortably propped in his deep chair, and with this beauty before his eyes, stayed with them.

The governess, a small corpulent middle-class woman with a red face, finally gave the sign to rise. With lifted brows, she pushed back her chair and bowed, as a large woman dressed in grey and richly jewelled with pearls entered the lobby. This woman was advancing with coolness and precision; her lightly powdered hair and the lines of her dress were arranged with the simplicity which always signifies taste in those quarters where devoutness is taken as one element of dignity. She might have been the wife of some high German official. Except that her jewellery added something fantastically lavish to her appearance; indeed, it was almost priceless, and consisted of ear pendants and a very long triple chain of softly glowing pearls, as large as cherries.

The children had risen promptly. They bent over to kiss the hand of their mother who, with a distant smile on her well preserved though somewhat tired and peaked features, looked over their heads and directed a few words to the governess in French. Then she walked to the glass door. The children followed her: the girls in the order of their age, after them the governess, the boy last. For some reason or other he turned around before crossing the sill, and since no one else was in the lobby his strange dusky eyes met those of Aschenbach who, his newspaper on his knees, lost in thought, was gazing after the group.

What he saw had not been unusual in the slightest detail. They had not preceded the mother to the table; they had waited, greeted her with respect, and observed the customary forms on entering the room. But it had taken place so pointedly, with such an accent of training, duty, and self-respect, that Aschenbach felt peculiarly touched by it all. He delayed for a few moments, then he too crossed into the dining-room, and was assigned to his table, which, as he noted with a brief touch of regret, was very far removed from that of the Polish family.

Weary, and yet intellectually active, he entertained himself during the lengthy meal with abstract, or even transcendental things; he thought over the secret union which the lawful must enter upon with the individual for human beauty to result, from this he passed into general problems of form and art, and at the end he found that his thoughts and discoveries were like the seemingly felicitous promptings of a dream which, when the mind is sobered, are seen to be completely empty and unfit. After the meal, smoking, sitting, taking an occasional turn in the park with its smell of nightfall, he went to bed early and spent the night in a sleep deep and unbroken, but often enlivened with the apparitions of dreams.

III (continued)

The weather did not improve any the following day. A land breeze was blowing. Under a cloudy ashen sky, the sea lay in dull peacefulness; it seemed shrivelled up, with a close dreary horizon, and it had retreated from the beach, baring the long ribs of several sandbanks. As Aschenbach opened his window he thought that he could detect the foul smell of the lagoon.

He felt depressed. He thought already of leaving. Once, years ago, after several weeks of spring here, this same weather had afflicted him, and impaired his health so seriously that he had to abandon Venice like a fugitive. Was not this old feverish unrest again setting in, the pressure in the temples, the heaviness of the eyelids? It would be annoying to change his residence still another time; but if the wind did not turn, he could not stay here. To be safe, he did not unpack completely. He breakfasted at nine in the buffet-room provided for this purpose between the lobby and the dining-room.

That formal silence reigned here which is the ambition of large hotels. The waiters who were serving walked about on soft soles. Nothing was audible but the tinkling of the tea-things, a word half-whispered. In one corner, obliquely across from the door, and two tables removed from his own, Aschenbach observed the Polish girls with their governess. Erect and red-eyed, their ash-blond hair freshly smoothed down, dressed in stiff blue linen with little white cuffs and turned-down collars—they were sitting there, handing around a glass of marmalade. They had almost finished their breakfast. The boy was missing.

Aschenbach smiled. "Well, little Phaeacian!" he thought. "You seem to be enjoying the pleasant privilege of having your sleep out." And suddenly exhilarated, he recited to himself the line: "A frequent change of dress; warm baths, and rest."

He breakfasted without haste. From the porter, who entered the hall holding his braided cap in his hand, he received some forwarded mail; and while he smoked a cigarette he opened a few letters. In this way it happened that he was present at the entrance of the late sleeper who was being waited for over yonder.

He came through the glass door and crossed the room in silence to his sisters' table. His approach—the way he held the upper part of his body, and bent his knees, the movement of his white-shod feet—had an extraordinary charm; he walked very lightly, at once timid and proud, and this became still more lovely through the childish embarrassment with which, twice as he proceeded, he turned his face towards the centre of the room, raising and lowering his eyes. Smiling, with something half-muttered in his soft vague tongue, he took his place; and now, as he turned his full profile to the observer, Aschenbach was again astonished, terrified even, by the really godlike beauty of this human child. To-day the boy was wearing a light blouse of blue and white striped cotton goods, with a red silk tie in front, and closed at the neck by a plain white high collar. This collar lacked the distinctiveness of the blouse, but above it the flowering head was poised with an incomparable seductiveness—the head of an Eros, in blended yellows of Parian marble, with fine serious brows, the temples and ears covered softly by the abrupt encroachment of his curls.

"Good, good!" Aschenbach thought, with that deliberate expert appraisal which artists sometimes employ as a subterfuge when they have been carried away with delight before a masterwork. And he thought further: "Really, if the sea and the beach weren't waiting for me, I should stay here as long as you stayed!" But he went then, passed through the lobby under the inspection of the servants, down the wide terrace, and straight across the boardwalk to the section of the beach reserved for the hotel guests. The barefoot old man in dungarees and straw hat who was functioning here as bathing master assigned him to the bath house he had rented; a table and a seat were placed on the sandy board platform, and he made himself comfortable in the lounge chair which he had drawn closer to the sea, out into the waxen yellow sand.

More than ever before he was entertained and amused by the sights on the beach, this spectacle of carefree, civilized people getting sensuous enjoyment at the very edge of the elements. The grey flat sea was already alive with wading children, swimmers, a motley of figures lying on the sandbanks with arms bent behind their heads. Others were rowing about in little red and blue striped boats without keels; they were continually upsetting, amid laughter. Before the long stretches of bathing houses, where people were sitting on the platforms as though on small verandahs, there was a play of movement against the line of rest and inertness behind—visits and chatter, fastidious morning elegance alongside the nakedness which, boldly at ease, was enjoying the freedom which the place afforded. Further in front, on the damp firm sand, people were parading about in white bathing cloaks, in ample, brilliantly coloured wrappers. An elaborate sand pile to the right, erected by children, had flags in the colours of all nations planted around it. Venders of shells, cakes, and fruit spread out their wares, kneeling. To the left, before one of the bathing houses which stood at right angles to the others and to the sea, a Russian family was encamped: men with beards and large teeth, slow delicate women, a Baltic girl sitting by an easel and painting the sea amidst exclamations of despair, two ugly good-natured children, an old maid-servant who wore a kerchief on her head and had the alert scraping manners of a slave. Delighted and appreciative, they were living there, patiently calling the names of the two rowdy disobedient children, using their scanty Italian to joke with the humorous old man from whom they were buying candy, kissing one another on the cheek, and not in the least concerned with any one who might be observing their community.

"Yes, I shall stay," Aschenbach thought. "Where would things be better?" And his hands folded in his lap, he let his eyes lose themselves in the expanses of the sea, his gaze gliding, swimming, and failing in the monotone mist of the wilderness of space. He loved the ocean for deep-seated reasons: because of that yearning for rest, when the hard-pressed artist hungers to shut out the exacting multiplicities of experience and hide himself on the breast of the simple, the vast; and because of a forbidden hankering—seductive, by virtue of its being directly opposed to his obligations—after the incommunicable, the incommensurate, the eternal, the non-existent. To be at rest in the face of perfection is the hunger of everyone who is aiming at excellence; and what is the non-existent but a form of perfection? But now, just as his dreams were so far out in vacancy, suddenly the horizontal fringe of the sea was broken by a human figure; and as he brought his eyes back from the unbounded, and focussed them, it was the lovely boy who was there, coming from the left and passing him on the sand. He was barefooted, ready for wading, his slender legs exposed above the knees; he walked slowly, but as lightly and proudly as though it were the customary thing for him to move about without shoes; and he was looking around him towards the line of bathing houses opposite. But as soon as he had noticed the Russian family, occupied with their own harmony and contentment, a cloud of scorn and detestation passed over his face. His brow darkened, his mouth was compressed, he gave his lips an embittered twist to one side so that the cheek was distorted, and the forehead became so heavily furrowed that the eyes seemed sunken beneath its pressure: malicious and glowering, they spoke the language of hate. He looked down, looked back once more threateningly, then with his shoulder made an abrupt gesture of disdain and dismissal, and left the enemy behind him.

A kind of pudency or confusion, something like respect and shyness, caused Aschenbach to turn away as though he had seen nothing. For the earnest-minded who have been casual observers of some passion, struggle against making use, even to themselves, of what they have seen. But he was both cheered and unstrung—which is to say, he was happy. This childish fanaticism, directed against the most good-natured possible aspect of life—it brought the divinely arbitrary into human relationships; it made a delightful natural picture which had appealed only to the eye now seem worthy of a deeper sympathy; and it gave the figure of this half-grown boy, who had already been important enough by his sheer beauty, something to offset him still further, and to make one take him more seriously than his years justified. Still looking away, Aschenbach could hear the boy's voice, the shrill, somewhat weak voice with which, in the distance now, he was trying to call hello to his playfellows busied around the sand pile. They answered him, shouting back his name, or some affectionate nickname; and Aschenbach listened with a certain curiosity, without being able to catch anything more definite than two melodic syllables like "Adgio," or still more frequently "Adgiu," with a ringing u-sound prolonged at the end. He was pleased with the resonance of this; he found it adequate to the subject. He repeated it silently and, satisfied, turned to his letters and manuscripts.

His small portable writing-desk on his knees he began writing with his fountain pen an answer to this or that bit of correspondence. But after the first fifteen minutes he found it a pity to abandon the situation—the most enjoyable he could think of—in this manner and waste it in activities which did not interest him. He tossed the writing materials to one side, and he faced the ocean again; soon afterwards, diverted by the childish voices around the sand heap, he revolved his head comfortably along the back of the chair towards the right, to discover where that excellent little Adgio might be and what he was doing.

He was found at a glance; the red tie on his breast was not to be overlooked. Busied with the others in laying an old plank across the damp moat of the sand castle, he was nodding, and shouting instructions for this work. There were about ten companions with him, boys and girls of his age, and a few younger ones who were chattering with one another in Polish, French, and in several Balkan tongues. But it was his name which rang out most often. He was openly in demand, sought after, admired. One boy especially, like him a Pole, a stocky fellow who was called something like "Jaschu," with sleek black hair and a belted linen coat, seemed to be his closest vassal and friend. When the work on the sand structure was finished for the time being, they walked aim in arm along the beach, and the boy who was called "Jaschu" kissed the beauty.

Aschenbach was half minded to raise a warning finger. "I advise you, Cristobulus," he thought, smiling, "to travel for a year! For you need that much time at least to get over it." And then he breakfasted on large ripe strawberries which he got from a peddler. It had become very warm, although the sun could no longer penetrate the blanket of mist in the sky. Laziness clogged his brain, even while his senses delighted in the numbing, drugging distractions of the ocean's stillness. To guess, to puzzle out just what name it was that sounded something like "Adgio," seemed to the sober man an appropriate ambition, a thoroughly comprehensive pursuit. And with the aid of a few scrappy recollections of Polish he decided that they must mean Tadzio, the shortened form of Tadeusz, and sounding like Tadziu when it is called.

Tadzio was bathing. Aschenbach, who had lost sight of him, spied his head and the arm with which he was propelling himself, far out in the water; for the sea must have been smooth for a long distance out. But already people seemed worried about him; women's voices were calling after him from the bathing houses, uttering this name again and again. It almost dominated the beach like a battle-cry, and with its soft consonants, its long drawn u-note at the end, it had something at once sweet and wild about it: "Tadziu! Tadziu!" He turned back; beating the resistent water into a foam with his legs he hurried, his head bent down over the waves. And to see how this living figure, graceful and clean-cut in its advance, with dripping curls, and lovely as some frail god, came up out of the depths of sky and sea, rose and separated from the elements—this spectacle aroused a sense of myth, it was like some poet's recovery of time at its beginning, of the origin of forms and the birth of gods. Aschenbach listened with closed eyes to this song ringing within him, and he thought again that it was pleasant here, and that he would like to remain.

Later Tadzio was resting from his bath; he lay in the sand, wrapped in his white robe, which was drawn under the right shoulder, his head supported on his bare arm. And even when Aschenbach was not observing him, but was reading a few pages in his book, he hardly ever forgot that this boy was lying there and that it would cost him only a slight turn of his head to the right to behold the mystery. It seemed that he was sitting here just to keep watch over his repose—busied with his own concerns, and yet constantly aware of this noble picture at his right, not far in the distance. And he was stirred by a paternal affection, the profound leaning which those who have devoted their thoughts to the creation of beauty feel towards those who possess beauty itself.

A little past noon he left the beach, returned to the hotel, and was taken up to his room. He stayed there for some time in front of the mirror, looking at his grey hair, his tired sharp features. At this moment he thought of his reputation, and of the fact that he was often recognized on the streets and observed with respect, thanks to the sure aim and the appealing finish of his words. He called up all the exterior successes of his talent which he could think of, remembering also his elevation to the knighthood. Then he went down to the dining-hall for lunch, and ate at his little table. As he was riding up in the lift, after the meal was ended, a group of young people just coming from breakfast pressed into the swaying cage after him, and Tadzio entered too. He stood quite near to Aschenbach, for the first time so near that Aschenbach could see him, not with the aloofness of a picture, but in minute detail, in all his human particularities. The boy was addressed by someone or other, and as he was answering with an indescribably agreeable smile he stepped out again, on the second floor, walking backwards, and with his eyes lowered. "Beauty makes modest," Aschenbach thought, and he tried insistently to explain why this was so. But he had noticed that Tadzio's teeth were not all they should be; they were somewhat jagged and pale. The enamel did not look healthy; it had a peculiar brittleness and transparency, as is often the case with anaemics. "He is very frail, he is sickly," Aschenbach thought. "In all probability he will not grow old." And he refused to reckon with the feeling of gratification or reassurance which accompanied this notion.

He spent two hours in his room, and in the afternoon he rode in the *vaporetto* across the foul-smelling lagoon to Venice. He got off at San Marco, took tea on the Piazza, and then, in accord with his schedule for the day, he went for a walk through the streets. Yet it was this walk which produced a complete reversal in his attitudes and his plans.

An offensive sultriness lay over the streets. The air was so heavy that the smells pouring out of homes, stores, and eating houses became mixed with oil, vapours, clouds of perfume, and still other odours—and these would not blow away, but hung in layers. Cigarette smoke remained suspended, disappearing very slowly. The crush of people along the narrow streets irritated rather than entertained the walker. The farther he went, the more he was depressed by the repulsive condition resulting from the combination of sea air and sirocco, which was at the same time both stimulating and enervating. He broke into an uncomfortable sweat. His eyes failed him, his chest became tight, he had a fever, the blood was pounding in his head. He fled from the crowded business streets across a bridge into the walks of the poor. On a quiet square, one of those forgotten and enchanting places which lie in the interior of Venice, he rested at the brink of a well, dried his forehead, and realized that he would have to leave here.

For the second and last time it had been demonstrated that this city in this kind of weather was decidedly unhealthy for him. It seemed foolish to attempt a stubborn resistance, while the prospects for a change of wind were completely uncertain. A quick decision was called for. It was not possible to go home this soon. Neither summer nor winter quarters were prepared to receive him. But this was not the only place where there were sea and beach; and elsewhere these could be found without the lagoon and its malarial mists. He remembered a little watering place not far from Trieste which had been praised to him. Why not there? And without delay, so that this new change of location would still have time to do him some good. He pronounced this as good as settled, and stood up. At the next gondola station he took a boat back to San Marco, and was led through the dreary labyrinth of canals, under fancy marble balconies flanked with lions, around the corners of smooth walls, past the sorrowing façades of palaces which mirrored large dilapidated business-signs in the pulsing water. He had trouble arriving there, for the gondolier, who was in league with lace-makers and glass-blowers, was always trying to land him for inspections and purchases; and just as the bizarre trip through Venice would begin to cast its spell, the greedy business sense of the sunken Queen did all it could to destroy the illusion.

When he had returned to the hotel he announced at the office before dinner that unforeseen developments necessitated his departure the following morning. He was assured of their regrets. He settled his accounts. He dined, and spent the warm evening reading the newspapers in a rocking-chair on the rear terrace. Before going to bed he got his luggage all ready for departure.

He did not sleep so well as he might, since the impending break-up made him restless. When he opened the window in the morning the sky was as overcast as ever, but the air seemed fresher, and he was already beginning to repent. Hadn't his decision been somewhat hasty and uncalled for, the result of a passing diffidence and indisposition? If he had delayed a little, if, instead of surrendering so easily, he had made some attempt to adjust himself to the air of Venice or to wait for an improvement in the weather, he would not be so rushed and inconvenienced, but could anticipate another forenoon on the beach like yesterday's. Too late. Now he would have to go on wanting what he had wanted yesterday. He dressed, and at about eight o'clock rode down to the ground floor for breakfast.

As he entered, the buffet-room was still empty of guests. A few came in while he sat waiting for his order. With his tea cup to his lips, he saw the Polish girls and their governess appear: rigid, with morning freshness, their eyes still red, they walked across to their table in the corner by the window. Immediately afterwards, the porter approached him, cap in hand, and warned him that it was time to go. The automobile is ready to take him and the other passengers to the Hotel Excelsior, and from here the motorboat will bring the ladies and gentlemen to the station through the company's private canal. Time is pressing.—Aschenbach found that it was doing nothing of the sort. It was still over an hour before his train left. He was irritated by this hotel custom of hustling departing guests out of the house, and indicated to the porter that he wished to finish his breakfast in peace. The man retired hesitatingly, to appear again five minutes later. It is impossible for the car to wait any longer. Then he would take a cab, and carry his trunk with him, Aschenbach replied in anger. He would use the public steamboat at the proper time, and he requested that it be left to him personally to worry about his departure. The employee bowed himself away. Pleased with the way he had warded off these importunate warnings, Aschenbach finished his meal at leisure; in fact, he even let the waiter bring him a newspaper. The time had become quite short when he finally arose. It was fitting that at the same moment Tadzio should come through the glass door.

On the way to his table he walked in the opposite direction to Aschenbach, lowering his eyes modestly before the man with the grey hair and high forehead, only to raise them again, in his delicious manner, soft and full upon him—and he had passed. "Good-bye, Tadzio!" Aschenbach thought. "I did not see much of you." He did what was unusual with him, really formed the words on his lips and spoke them to himself; then he added, "God bless you!"—After this he left, distributed tips, was ushered out by the small gentle manager in the French frock coat, and made off from the hotel on foot, as he had come, going along the white blossoming avenue which crossed the island to the steamer bridge, accompanied by the house servant carrying his hand luggage. He arrived, took his place—and then followed a painful journey through all the depths of regret.

It was the familiar trip across the lagoon, past San Marco, up the Grand Canal. Aschenbach sat on the circular bench at the bow, his arm supported against the railing, shading his eyes with his hand. The public gardens were left behind, the Piazzetta opened up once more in princely splendour and was gone, then came the great flock of palaces, and as the channel made a turn the magnificently slung marble arch of the Rialto came into view. The traveller was watching; his emotions were in conflict. The atmosphere of the city, this slightly foul smell of sea and swamp which he had been so anxious to avoid—he breathed it now in deep, exquisitely painful draughts. Was it possible that he had not known, had not considered, just how much he was attached to all this? What had been a partial misgiving this morning, a faint doubt as to the advisability of his move, now became a distress, a positive misery, a spiritual hunger, and so bitter that it frequently brought tears to his eyes, while he told himself that he could not possibly have foreseen it. Hardest of all to bear, at times completely insufferable, was the thought that he would never see Venice again, that this was a leave-taking for ever. Since it had been shown for the second time that the city affected his health, since he was compelled for the second time to get away in all haste, from now on he would have to consider it a place impossible and forbidden to him, a place which he was not equal to, and which it would be foolish for him to visit again. Yes, he felt that if he left now, he would be shamefaced and defiant enough never to see again the beloved city which had twice caused him a physical break-down. And of a sudden this struggle between his desires and his physical strength seemed to the aging man so grave and important, his physical defeat seemed so dishonourable, so much a challenge to hold out at any cost, that he could not understand the ready submissiveness of the day before, when he had decided to give in without attempting any serious resistance.

Meanwhile the steamboat was nearing the station; pain and perplexity increased, he became distracted. In his affliction, he felt that it was impossible to leave, and just as impossible to turn back. The conflict was intense as he entered the station. It was very late; there was not a moment to lose if he was to catch the train. He wanted to, and he did not want to. But time was pressing; it drove him on. He hurried to get his ticket, and looked about in the tumult of the hall for the officer on duty here from the hotel. The man appeared and announced that the large trunk had been transferred. Transferred already? Yes, thank you—to Como. To Como? And in the midst of hasty running back and forth, angry questions and confused answers, it came to light that the trunk had already been sent with other foreign baggage from the express office of the Hotel Excelsior in a completely wrong direction.

Aschenbach had difficulty in preserving the expression which was required under these circumstances. He was almost convulsed with an adventurous delight, an unbelievable hilarity. The employee rushed off to see if it were still possible to stop the trunk, and as was to be expected he returned with nothing accomplished. Aschenbach declared that he did not want to travel without his trunk, but had decided to go back and wait at the beach hotel for its return. Was the company's motorboat still at the station? The man assured him that it was lying at the door. With Italian volubility he persuaded the clerk at the ticket window to redeem the cancelled ticket, he swore that they would act speedily, that no time or money would be spared in recovering the trunk promptly, and—so the strange thing happened that, twenty minutes after his arrival at the station, the traveller found himself again on the Grand Canal, returning to the Lido.

Here was an adventure, wonderful, abashing, and comically dreamlike beyond belief: places which he had just bid farewell to for ever in the most abject misery—yet he had been turned and driven back by fate, and was seeing them again in the same hour! The spray from the bow, washing between gondolas and steamers with an absurd agility, shot the speedy little craft ahead to its goal, while the one passenger was hiding the nervousness and ebullience of a truant boy under the mask of resigned anger. From time to time he shook with laughter at this mishap which, as he told himself, could not have turned out better for a child of destiny. There were explanations to be given, expressions of astonishment to be faced—and then, he told himself, everything would be all right; then a misfortune would be avoided, a grave error rectified. And all that he had thought he was leaving behind him would be open to him again, there at his disposal. . . . And to cap it all, was the rapidity of the ride deceiving him, or was the wind really coming from the sea?

The waves beat against the walls of the narrow canal which runs through the island to the Hotel Excelsior. An automobile omnibus was awaiting his return there, and took him above the rippling sea straight to the beach hotel. The little manager with moustache and long-tailed frock coat came down the stairs to meet him.

He ingratiatingly regretted the episode, spoke of it as highly painful to him and the establishment, but firmly approved of Aschenbach's decision to wait here for the baggage. Of course his room had been given up, but there was another one, just as good, which he could occupy immediately. "*Pas de chance, Monsieur*," the Swiss elevator boy smiled as they were ascending. And so the fugitive was established again, in a room almost identical to the other in its location and furnishings.

Tired out by the confusion of this strange forenoon, he distributed the contents of his hand-bag about the room and dropped into an arm-chair by the open window. The sea had become a pale green, the air seemed thinner and purer; the beach, with its cabins and boats, seemed to have colour, although the sky was still grey. Aschenbach looked out, his hands folded in his lap; he was content to be back, but shook his head disapprovingly at his irresolution, his failure to know his own mind. He sat here for the better part of an hour, resting and dreaming vaguely. About noon he saw Tadzio in a striped linen suit with a red tie, coming back from the sea across the private beach and along the boardwalk to the hotel. Aschenbach recognized him from this altitude before he had actually set eyes on him; he was about to think some such words as "Well, Tadzio, there you are again!" but at the same moment he felt this careless greeting go dumb before the truth in his heart. He felt the exhilaration of his blood, a conflict of pain and pleasure, and he realized that it was Tadzio who had made it so difficult for him to leave.

He sat very still, entirely unobserved from this height, and looked within himself. His features were alert, his eyebrows raised, and an attentive, keenly inquisitive smile distended his mouth. Then he raised his head; lifted both hands, which had hung relaxed over the arms of the chair, and in a slow twisting movement turned the palms downward—as though to suggest an opening and spreading outward of his arms. It was a spontaneous act of welcome, of calm acceptance.

IV

Day after day now the naked god with the hot cheeks drove his fire-breathing quadriga across the expanses of the sky, and his yellow locks fluttered in the assault of the east wind. A white silk sheen stretched over the slowly simmering Ponto. The sand glowed. Beneath the quaking silver blue of the ether rust-coloured canvasses were spread in front of the beach bathing houses, and the afternoons were spent in the sharply demarcated spots of shade which they cast. But it was also delightful in the evening, when the vegetation in the park had the smell of balsam, and the stars were working through their courses above, and the soft persistent murmur of the sea came up enchantingly through the night. Such evenings contained the cheering promise that more sunny days of casual idleness would follow, dotted with countless closely interspersed possibilities of well-timed accidents.

The guest who was detained here by such an accommodating mishap did not consider the return of his property as sufficient grounds for another departure. He suffered some inconvenience for two days, and had to appear for meals in the large dining-room in his travelling clothes. When the strayed luggage was finally deposited in his room again, he unpacked completely and filled the closet and drawers with his belongings; he had decided to remain here indefinitely, content now that he could pass the hours on the beach in a silk suit and appear for dinner at his little table again in appropriate evening dress.

The comfortable rhythm of this life had already cast its spell over him; he was soon enticed by the ease, the mild splendour, of his programme. Indeed, what a place to be in, when the usual allurement of living in watering places on southern shores was coupled with the immediate nearness of the most wonderful of all cities! Aschenbach was not a lover of pleasure. Whenever that was some call for him to take a holiday, to indulge himself, to have a good time—and this was especially true at an earlier age—restlessness and repugnance soon drove him back to his rigorous toil, the faithful sober efforts of his daily routine. Except that this place was bewitching him, relaxing his will, making him happy. In the mornings, under the shelter of his bathing house, letting his eyes roam dreamily in the blue of the southern sea; or on a warm night as he leaned back against the cushions of the gondola carrying him under the broad starry sky home to the Lido from the Piazza di San Marco after long hours of idleness—and the brilliant lights, the melting notes of the serenade were being left behind—he often recalled his place in the mountains, the scene of his battles in the summer, where the clouds blew low across his garden, and terrifying storms put out the lamps at night, and the crows which he fed were swinging in the tops of the pine trees. Then everything seemed just right to him, as though he were lifted into the Elysian fields, on the borders of the earth, where man enjoys the easiest life, where there is no snow or winter, nor storms and pouring rains, but where Oceanus continually sends forth gentle cooling breezes, and the days pass in a blessed inactivity, without work, without effort, devoted wholly to the sun and to the feast days of the sun.

Aschenbach saw the boy Tadzio frequently, almost constantly. Owing to the limited range of territory and the regularity of their lives, the beauty was near him at short intervals throughout the day. He saw him, met him, everywhere: in the lower rooms of the hotel, on the cooling water trips to the city and back, in the arcades of the square, and at times when he was especially lucky ran across him on the streets. But principally, and with the most gratifying regularity, the forenoon on the beach allowed him to admire and study this rare spectacle at his leisure. Yes, it was this guaranty of happiness, this daily recurrence of good fortune, which made his stay here so precious, and gave him such pleasure in the constant procession of sunny days.

He was up as early as he used to be when under the driving pressure of work, and was on the beach before most people, when the sun was still mild and the sea lay blinding white in the dreaminess of morning. He spoke amiably to the guard of the private beach, and also spoke familiarly to the barefoot, white-bearded old man who had prepared his place for him, stretching the brown canopy and bringing the furniture of the cabin out on the platform. Then he took his seat. There would now be three or four hours in which the sun mounted and gained terrific strength, the sea a deeper and deeper blue, and he might look at Tadzio.

He saw him approaching from the left, along the edge of the sea; he saw him as he stepped out backwards from among the cabins; or he would suddenly find, with a shock of pleasure, that he had missed his coming, that he was already here in the blue and white bathing suit which was his only garment now while on the beach, that he had already commenced his usual activities in the sun and the sand—a pleasantly trifling, idle, and unstable manner of living, a mixture of rest and play. Tadzio would saunter about, wade, dig, catch things, lie down, go for a swim, all the while being kept under surveillance by the women on the platform who made his name ring out in their falsetto voices: "Tadziu! Tadziu!" Then he would come running to them with a look of eagerness, to tell them what he had seen, what he had experienced, or to show them what he had found or caught: mussels, sea-horses, jelly-fish, and crabs that ran sideways. Aschenbach did not understand a word he said, and though it might have been the most ordinary thing in the world, it was a vague harmony in his ear. So the foreignness of the boy's speech turned it into music, a wanton sun poured its prodigal splendour down over him, and his figure was always set off against the background of an intense sea-blue.

This piquant body was so freely exhibited that his eyes soon knew every line and posture. He was continually rediscovering with new pleasure all this familiar beauty, and his astonishment at its delicate appeal to his senses was unending. The boy was called to greet a guest who was paying his respects to the ladies at the bathing house. He came running, running wet perhaps out of the water, tossed back his curls, and as he held out his hand, resting on one leg and raising his other foot on the toes, the set of his body was delightful; it had a charming expectancy about it, a well-meaning shyness, a winsomeness which showed his aristocratic training. . . . He lay stretched full length, his bath towel slung across his shoulders, his delicately chiselled arm supported in the sand, his chin in his palm; the boy called Jaschu was squatting near him and making up to him—and nothing could be more enchanting than the smile of his eyes and lips when the leader glanced up at his inferior, his servant. . . . He stood on the edge of the sea, alone, apart from his people, quite near to Aschenbach—erect, his hands locked across the back of his neck, he swayed slowly on the balls of his feet, looked dreamily into the blueness of sea and sky, while tiny waves rolled up and bathed his feet. His honey-coloured hair clung in rings about his neck and temples. The sun made the down on his back glitter; the fine etching of the ribs, the symmetry of the chest, were emphasized by the tightness of the suit across the buttocks. His arm-pits were still as smooth as those of a statue; the hollows of his knees glistened, and their bluish veins made his body seem built of some clearer stuff. What rigour, what precision of thought, were expressed in this erect, youthfully perfect body! Yet the pure and strenuous will which, darkly at work, could bring such godlike sculpture to the light— was not he, the artist, familiar with this? Did it not operate in him too when he, under the press of frugal passions, would free from the marble mass of speech some slender form which he had seen in the mind and which he put before his fellows as a statue and a mirror of intellectual beauty?

Statue and mirror! His eyes took in the noble form there bordered with blue; and with a rush of enthusiasm he felt that in this spectacle he was catching the beautiful itself, form as the thought of God, the one pure perfection which lives in the mind, and which, in this symbol and likeness, had been placed here quietly and simply as an object of devotion. That was drunkenness; and eagerly, without thinking, the aging artist welcomed it. His mind was in travail; all that he had learned, dropped back into flux; his understanding threw up age-old thoughts which he had inherited with youth though they had never before lived with their own fire. Is it not written that the sun diverts our attention from intellectual to sensual things? Reason and understanding, it is said, become so numbed and enchanted that the soul forgets everything out of delight with its immediate circumstances, and in astonishment becomes attached to the most beautiful object shined on by the sun; indeed, only with the aid of a body is it capable then of raising itself to higher considerations. To be sure, Amor did as the instructors of mathematics who show backward children tangible representations of the pure forms—similarly the god, in order to make the spiritual visible for us, readily utilized the form and colour of man's youth, and as a reminder he adorned these with the reflected splendour of beauty which, when we behold it, makes us flare up in pain and hope.

His enthusiasm suggested these things, put him in the mood for them. And from the noise of the sea and the lustre of the sun he wove himself a charming picture. Here was the old plane-tree, not far from the walls of Athens—a holy, shadowy place filled with the smell of *agnus castus* blossoms and decorated with ornaments and images sacred to Achelous and the Nymphs. Clear and pure, the brook at the foot of the spreading tree fell across the smooth pebbles; the cicadas were fiddling. But on the grass, which was like a pillow gently sloping to the head, two people were stretched out, in hiding from the heat of the day: an older man and a youth, one ugly and one beautiful, wisdom next to loveliness. And amid gallantries and skilfully engaging banter, Socrates was instructing Phaedrus in matters of desire and virtue. He spoke to him of the hot terror which the initiate suffer when their eyes light on an image of the eternal beauty; spoke of the greed of the impious and the wicked who cannot think beauty when they see its likeness, and who are incapable of reverence; spoke of the holy distress which befalls the noble-minded when a godlike countenance, a perfect body, appears before them; they tremble and grow distracted, and hardly dare to raise their eyes, and they honour the man who possesses this beauty, yes, if they were not afraid of being thought downright madmen they would sacrifice to the beloved as to the image of a god. For beauty, my Phaedrus, beauty alone is both lovely and visible at once; it is, mark me, the only form of the spiritual which we can receive through the senses. Else what would become of us if the divine, if reason and virtue and truth, should appear to us through the senses? Should we not perish and be consumed with love, as Semele once was with Zeus? Thus, beauty is the sensitive man's access to the spirit—but only a road, a means simply, little Phaedrus. . . . And then this crafty suitor made the neatest remark of all; it was this, that the lover is more divine than the beloved, since the god is in the one, but not in the other—perhaps the most delicate, the most derisive thought which has ever been framed, and the one from which spring all the cunning and the profoundest pleasures of desire.

Writers are happiest with an idea which can become all emotion, and an emotion all idea. Just such a pulsating idea, such a precise emotion, belonged to the lonely man at this moment, was at his call. Nature, it ran, shivers with ecstasy when the spirit bows in homage before beauty. Suddenly he wanted to write. Eros loves idleness, they say, and he is suited only to idleness. But at this point in the crisis the affliction became a stimulus towards productivity. The incentive hardly mattered. A request, an agitation for an open statement on a certain large burning issue of culture and taste, was going about the intellectual world, and had finally caught up with the traveller here. He was familiar with the subject, it had touched his own experience; and suddenly he felt an irresistible desire to display it in the light of his own version. And he even went so far as to prefer working in Tadzio's presence, taking the scope of the boy as a standard for his writing, making his style follow the lines of this body which seemed godlike to him, and carrying his beauty over into the spiritual just as the eagle once carried the Trojan stag up into the ether. Never had his joy in words been more sweet. He had never been so aware that Eros is in the word as during those perilously precious hours when, at his crude table under the canopy, facing the idol and listening to the music of his voice, he followed Tadzio's beauty in the forming of his little tract, a page and a half of choice prose which was soon to excite the admiration of many through its clarity, its poise, and the vigorous curve of its emotion. Certainly it is better for people to know only the beautiful product as finished, and not in its conception, its conditions of origin. For knowledge of the sources from which the artist derives his inspiration would often confuse and alienate, and in this way detract from the effects of his mastery. Strange hours! Strangely enervating efforts! Rare creative intercourse between the spirit and a body! When Aschenbach put away his work and started back from the beach be felt exhausted, or in dispersion even; and it was as though his conscience were complaining after some transgression.

The following morning, as he was about to leave the hotel, he looked off from the steps and noticed that Tadzio, who was alone and was already on his way towards the sea, was just approaching the private beach. He was half tempted by the simple notion of seizing this opportunity to strike up a casual friendly acquaintanceship with the boy who had been the unconscious source of so much agitation and upheaval; he wanted to address him, and enjoy the answering look in his eyes. The boy was sauntering along, he could be overtaken; and Aschenbach quickened his pace. He reached him on the boardwalk behind the bathing houses; was about to lay a hand on his head and shoulders; and some word or other, an amiable phrase in French, was on the tip of his tongue. But he felt that his heart, due also perhaps to his rapid stride, was beating like a hammer; and he was so short of breath that his voice would have been tight and trembling. He hesitated, he tried to get himself under control. Suddenly he became afraid that he had been walking too long so close behind the boy. He was afraid of arousing curiosity and causing him to look back questioningly. He made one more spurt, failed, surrendered, and passed with bowed head.

"Too late!" he thought immediately. Too late! Yet was it too late? This step which he had just been on the verge of taking would very possibly have put things on a sound, free and easy basis, and would have restored him to wholesome soberness. But the fact was that Aschenbach did not want soberness: his intoxication was too precious. Who can explain the stamp and the nature of the artist! Who can understand this deep instinctive welding of discipline and licence? For to be unable to want wholesome soberness, is licence. Aschenbach was no longer given to self-criticism. His tastes, the mental caliber of his years, his self-respect, ripeness, and a belated simplicity made him unwilling to dismember his motives and to debate whether his impulses were the result of conscientiousness or of dissolution and weakness. He was embarrassed, as he feared that someone or other, if only the guard on the beach, must have observed his pursuit and defeat. He was very much afraid of the ridiculous. Further, he joked with himself about his comically pious distress. "Downed," he thought, "downed like a rooster, with his wings hanging miserably in the battle. It really is a god who can, at one sight of his loveliness, break our courage this way and force down our pride so thoroughly. . . ." He toyed and skirmished with his emotions, and was far too haughty to be afraid of them.

He had already ceased thinking about the time when the vacation period which he had fixed for himself would expire; the thought of going home never even suggested itself. He had sent for an ample supply of money. His only concern was with the possible departure of the Polish family; by a casual questioning of the hotel barber he had contrived to learn that these people had come here only a short time before his own arrival. The sun browned his face and hands, the invigorating salt breezes made him feel fresher. Once he had been in the habit of expending on his work every bit of nourishment which food, sleep, or nature could provide him; and similarly now he was generous and uneconomical, letting pass off as elation and emotion all the daily strengthening derived from sun, idleness, and sea air.

His sleep was fitful; the preciously uniform days were separated by short nights of happy unrest. He did retire early, for at nine o'clock, when Tadzio had disappeared from the scene, the day seemed over. But at the first grey of dawn he was awakened by a gently insistent shock; he suddenly remembered his adventure, he could no longer remain in bed; he arose, and clad lightly against the chill of morning, he sat down by the open window to await the rising of the sun. Revived by his sleep, he watched this miraculous event with reverence. Sky, earth, and sea still lay in glassy, ghost-like twilight; a dying star still floated in the emptiness of space But a breeze started up, a winged message from habitations beyond reach, telling that Eros was rising from beside her husband. And that first sweet reddening in the farthest stretches of sky and sea took place by which the sentiency of creation is announced.

The goddess was approaching, the seductress of youth who stole Cleitus and Cephalus, and despite the envy of all the Olympians enjoyed the love of handsome Orion. A strewing of roses began there on the edge of the world, an unutterably pure glowing and blooming. Childish clouds, lighted and shined through, floated like busy little Cupids in the rosy, bluish mist. Purple fell upon the sea, which seemed to be simmering, and washing the colour towards him. Golden spears shot up into the sky from behind. The splendour caught fire, silently, and with godlike power an intense flame of licking tongues broke out—and with rattling hoofs the brother's sacred chargers mounted the horizon. Lighted by the god's brilliance, he sat there, keeping watch alone. He closed his eyes, letting this glory play against the lids. Past emotions, precious early afflictions and yearnings which had been stifled by his rigorous programme of living, were now returning in such strange new forms. With an embarrassed, astonished smile, he recognized them. He was thinking, dreaming; slowly his lips formed a name. And still smiling, with his face turned upwards, hands folded in his lap, he fell asleep again in his chair.

But the day which began with such fiery solemnity underwent a strange mythical transformation. Where did the breeze originate which suddenly began playing so gently and insinuatingly, like some whispered suggestion, about his ears and temples? Little white choppy clouds stood in the sky in scattered clumps, like the pasturing herds of the gods. A stronger wind arose, and the steeds of Poseidon came prancing up, and along with them the steers which belonged to the blue-locked god, bellowing and lowering their horns as they ran. Yet among the detritus of the more distant beach waves were hopping forward like agile goats. He was caught in the enchantment of a sacredly distorted world full of Panic life—and he dreamed delicate legends. Often, when the sun was sinking behind Venice, he would sit on a bench in the park observing Tadzio who was dressed in a white suit with a coloured sash and was playing ball on the smooth gravel—and it was Hyacinth that he seemed to be watching. Hyacinth who was to die because two gods loved him. Yes, he felt Zephyr's aching jealousy of the rival who forgot the oracle, the bow, and the lyre, in order to play for ever with this beauty. He saw the discus, guided by a pitiless envy, strike the lovely head; he too, growing pale, caught the drooping body—and the flower, sprung from this sweet blood, bore the inscription of his unending grief.

Nothing is more unusual and strained than the relationship between people who know each other only with their eyes, who meet daily, even hourly, and yet are compelled, by force of custom or their own caprices, to say no word or make no move of acknowledgement, but to maintain the appearance of an aloof unconcern. There is a restlessness and a surcharged curiosity existing between them, the hysteria of an unsatisfied, unnaturally repressed desire for acquaintanceship and intercourse; and especially there is a kind of tense respect. For one person loves and honours another so long as he cannot judge him, and desire is an evidence of incomplete knowledge.

Some kind of familiarity had necessarily to form itself between Aschenbach and young Tadzio; and it gave the elderly man keen pleasure to see that his sympathies and interests were not left completely unanswered. For example, when the boy appeared on the beach in the morning and was going towards his family's bathing house, what had induced him never to use the boardwalk on the far side of it any more, but to stroll along the front path, through the sand, past Aschenbach's habitual place, and often unnecessarily close to him, almost touching his table, or his chair even? Did the attraction, the fascination of an overpowering emotion have such an effect upon the frail unthinking object of it? Aschenbach watched daily for Tadzio to approach; and sometimes he acted as though he were occupied when this event was taking place, and he let the boy pass unobserved. But at other times he would look up, and their glances met. They were both in deep earnest when this occurred. Nothing in the elderly man's cultivated and dignified expression betrayed any inner movement; but there was a searching look in Tadzio's eyes, a thoughtful questioning—he began to falter, looked down, then looked up again charmingly, and when he had passed something in his bearing seemed to indicate that it was only his breeding which kept him from turning around.

Once, however, one evening, things turned out differently. The Polish children and their governess had been missing at dinner in the large hall; Aschenbach had noted this uneasily. After the meal, disturbed by their absence, Aschenbach was walking in evening dress and straw hat in front of the hotel at the foot of the terrace, when suddenly he saw the nunlike sisters appear in the light of the arc-lamp, accompanied by their governess and with Tadzio a few steps behind. Evidently they were coming from the steamer pier after having dined for some reason in the city. It must have been cool on the water; Tadzio was wearing a dark blue sailor overcoat with gold buttons, and on his head he had a cap to match. The sun and sea air had not browned him; his skin still had the same yellow marble colour as at first. It even seemed paler to-day than usual, whether from the coolness or from the blanching moonlight of the lamps. His regular eyebrows showed up more sharply, the darkness of his eyes was deeper. It is hard to say how beautiful he was; and Aschenbach was distressed, as he had often been before, by the thought that words can only evaluate sensuous beauty, but not re-give it.

He had not been prepared for this rich spectacle; it came unhoped for. He had no time to entrench himself behind an expression of repose and dignity. Pleasure, surprise, admiration must have shown on his face as his eyes met those of the boy—and at this moment it happened that Tadzio smiled, smiled to him, eloquently, familiarly, charmingly, without concealment; and during the smile his lips slowly opened. It was the smile of Narcissus bent over the reflecting water, that deep, fascinated, magnetic smile with which he stretches out his arms to the image of his own beauty—a smile distorted ever so little, distorted at the hopelessness of his efforts to kiss the pure lips of the shadow. It was coquettish, inquisitive, and slightly tortured. It was infatuated, and infatuating.

He had received this smile, and he hurried away as though he carried a fatal gift. He was so broken up that he was compelled to escape the light of the terrace and the front garden; he hastily hunted out the darkness of the park in the rear. Strangely indignant and tender admonitions wrung themselves out of him: "You dare not smile like that! Listen, no one dare smile like that to another!" He threw himself down on a bench; in a frenzy he breathed the night smell of the vegetation. And leaning back, his arms loose, overwhelmed, with frequent chills running through him, he whispered the fixed formula of desire—impossible in this case, absurd, abject, ridiculous, and yet holy, even in this case venerable: "I love you!"

V

During his fourth week at the Lido Gustav von Aschenbach made several sinister observations touching on the world about him. First, it seemed to him that as the season progressed the number of guests at the hotel was diminishing rather than increasing; and German especially seemed to be dropping away, so that finally he heard nothing but foreign sounds at table and on the beach. Then one day in conversation with the barber, whom he visited often, he caught a word which startled him. The man had mentioned a German family that left soon after their arrival; he added glibly and flatteringly, "But you are staying, sir. You have no fear of the plague." Aschenbach looked at him. "The plague?" he repeated. The gossiper was silent, made out as though busy with other things, ignored the question. When it was put more insistently, he declared that he knew nothing, and with embarrassing volubility he tried to change the subject.

That was about noon. In the afternoon there was a calm, and Aschenbach rode to Venice under an intense sun. For he was driven by a mania to follow the Polish children whom he had seen with their governess taking the road to the steamer pier. He did not find the idol at San Marco. But while sitting over his tea at his little round iron table on the shady side of the square, he suddenly detected a peculiar odour in the air which, it seemed to him now, he had noticed for days without being consciously aware of it. The smell was sweetish and drug-like, suggesting sickness, and wounds, and a suspicious cleanliness. He tested and examined it thoughtfully, finished his luncheon, and left the square on the side opposite the church. The smell was stronger where the street narrowed. On the corners printed posters were hung, giving municipal warnings against certain diseases of the gastric system liable to occur at this season, against the eating of oysters and clams, and also against the water of the canals. The euphemistic nature of the announcement was palpable. Groups of people had collected in silence on the bridges and squares; and the foreigner stood among them, scenting and investigating.

At a little shop he inquired about the fatal smell, asking the proprietor, who was leaning against his door surrounded by coral chains and imitation amethyst jewellery. The man measured him with heavy eyes, and brightened up hastily. "A matter of precaution, sir!" he answered with a gesture. "A regulation of the police which must be taken for what it is worth. This weather is oppressive, the sirocco is not good for the health. In short, you understand—an exaggerated prudence perhaps." Aschenbach thanked him and went on. Also on the steamer back to the Lido he caught the smell of the disinfectant.

Returning to the hotel, he went immediately to the periodical stand in the lobby and ran through the papers. He found nothing in the foreign language press. The domestic press spoke of rumours, produced hazy statistics, repeated official denials and questioned their truthfulness. This explained the departure of the German and Austrian guests. Obviously, the subjects of the other nations knew nothing, suspected nothing, were not yet uneasy. "To keep it quiet!" Aschenbach thought angrily, as he threw the papers back on the table. "To keep that quiet!" But at the same moment he was filled with satisfaction over the adventure that was to befall the world about him. For passion, like crime, is not suited to the secure daily rounds of order and well-being; and every slackening in the bourgeois structure, every disorder and affliction of the world, must be held welcome, since they bring with them a vague promise of advantage. So Aschenbach felt a dark contentment with what was taking place, under cover of the authorities, in the dirty alleys of Venice. This wicked secret of the city was welded with his own secret, and he too was involved in keeping it hidden. For in his infatuation he cared about nothing but the possibility of Tadzio's leaving, and he realized with something like terror that he would not know how to go on living if this occurred.

Lately he had not been relying simply on good luck and the daily routine for his chances to be near the boy and look at him. He pursued him, stalked him. On Sundays, for instance, the Poles never appeared on the beach. He guessed that they must be attending mass at San Marco. He hurried there; and stepping from the heat of the square into the golden twilight of the church, he found the boy he was hunting, bowed over a *prie-dieu*, praying. Then he stood in the background, on the cracked mosaic floor, with people on all sides kneeling, murmuring, and making the sign of the cross. And the compact grandeur of this oriental temple weighed heavily on his senses. In front, the richly ornamented priest was conducting the office, moving about and singing; incense poured forth, clouding the weak little flame of the candle on the altar—and with the sweet, stuffy sacrificial odour another seemed to commingle faintly: the smell of the infested city. But through the smoke and the sparkle Aschenbach saw how the boy there in front turned his head, hunted him out, and looked at him.

When the crowd was streaming out through the opened portals into the brilliant square with its swarms of pigeons, the lover hid in the vestibule; he kept trader cover, he lay in wait. He saw the Poles quit the church, saw how the children took ceremonious leave of their mother, and how she turned towards the Piazzetta on her way home. He made sure that the boy, the nunlike sisters, and the governess took the road to the right through the gateway of the dock tower and into the Merceria. And after giving them a slight start, he followed, followed them furtively on their walk through

Venice. He had to stand still when they stopped, had to take flight in shops and courts to let them pass when they turned back. He lost them; hot and exhausted, he hunted them over bridges and down dirty blind-alleys—and he underwent minutes of deadly agony when suddenly he saw them coming towards him in a narrow passage where escape was impossible. Yet it could not be said that he suffered. He was drunk, and his steps followed the promptings of the demon who delights in treading human reason and dignity under foot.

In one place Tadzio and his companions took a gondola; and shortly after they had pushed off from the shore, Aschenbach, who had hidden behind some structure, a well, while they were climbing in, now did the same. He spoke in a hurried undertone as he directed the rower, with the promise of a generous tip, to follow unnoticed and at a distance that gondola which was just rounding the corner. And he thrilled when the man, with the roguish willingness of an accomplice, assured him in the same tone that his wishes would be carried out, carried out faithfully.

Leaning back against the soft black cushions, he rocked and glided towards the other black-beaked craft where his passion was drawing him. At times it escaped; then he felt worried and uneasy. But his pilot, as though skilled in such commissions, was always able through sly manoeuvres, speedy diagonals and shortcuts, to bring the quest into view again. The air was quiet and smelly, the sun burned down strong through the slate-coloured mist. Water slapped against the wood and stone. The call of the gondolier, half warning, half greeting, was answered with a strange obedience far away in the silence of the labyrinth. White and purple umbels with the scent of almonds hung down from little elevated gardens over crumbling walls. Arabian window-casings were outlined through the murkiness. The marble steps of a church descended into the water; a beggar squatted there, protesting his misery, holding out his hat, and showing the whites of his eyes as though he were blind. An antiquarian in front of his den fawned on the passer-by and invited him to stop in the hopes of swindling him. That was Venice, the flatteringly and suspiciously beautiful—this city, half legend, half snare for strangers; in its foul air art once flourished gluttonously, and had suggested to its musicians seductive notes which cradle and lull. The adventurer felt as though his eyes were taking in this same luxury, as though his ears were being won by just such melodies. He recalled too that the city was diseased and was concealing this through greed—and he peered more eagerly after the retreating gondola.

Thus, in his infatuation, he wanted simply to pursue uninterrupted the object that aroused him, to dream of it when it was not there, and, after the fashion of lovers, to speak softly to its mere outline. Loneliness, strangeness, and the joy of a deep belated intoxication encouraged him and prompted him to accept even the remotest things without reserve or shame—with the result that as he returned late in the evening from Venice, he stopped on the second floor of the hotel before the door of the boy's room, laid his head in utter drunkenness against the hinge of the door, and for a long time could not drag himself away despite the danger of being caught and embarrassed in such a mad situation.

Yet there were still moments of relief when he came partly to his senses. "Where to!" he would think, alarmed. "Where to!" Like every man whose natural abilities stimulate an aristocratic interest in his ancestry, he was accustomed to think of his forbears in connexion with the accomplishments and successes of his life, to assure himself of their approval, their satisfaction, their undeniable respect. He thought of them now, entangled as he was in such an illicit experience, caught in such exotic transgressions. He thought of their characteristic rigidity of principle, their scrupulous masculinity—and he smiled dejectedly. What would they say? But then, what would they have said to his whole life, which was almost degenerate in its departure from theirs, this life under the bane of art—a life against which he himself had once issued such youthful mockeries out of loyalty to his fathers, but which at bottom had been so much like theirs! He too had served, he too had been a soldier and a warrior like many of them—for art was a war, a destructive battle, and one was not equal to it for long these days. A life of self-conquest and of in-spite-offs, a rigid, sober, and unyielding life which he had formed into the symbol of a delicate and timely heroism. He might well call it masculine, or brave; and it almost seemed as though the Eros mastering him were somehow peculiarly adapted and inclined to such a life. Had not this Eros stood in high repute among the bravest of peoples; was it not true that precisely through bravery he had flourished in their cities? Numerous war heroes of antiquity had willingly borne his yoke, for nothing was deemed a disgrace which the god imposed; and acts which would Have been rebuked as the sign of cowardice if they had been done for other purposes—prostrations, oaths, entreaties, abjectness—such things did not bring shame upon the lover, but rather he reaped praise for them.

In this way his infatuation determined the course of his thoughts, in this way he tried to uphold himself, to preserve his respect. But at the same time, selfish and calculating, he turned his attention to the unclean transactions here in Venice, this adventure of the outer world which conspired darkly with his own and which fed his passion with vague lawless hopes.

Bent on getting reliable news of the condition and progress of the pestilence, he ransacked the local papers in the city cafés, as they had been missing from the reading table of the hotel lobby for several days now. Statements alternated with disavowals. The number of the sick and dead was supposed to reach twenty, forty, or even a hundred and more—and immediately afterwards every instance of the plague would be either flatly denied or attributed to completely isolated cases which had crept in from the outside. There were scattered admonitions, protests against the dangerous conduct of foreign authorities. Certainty was impossible. Nevertheless the lone man felt especially entitled to participate in the secret; and although he was excluded, he derived a grotesque satisfaction from putting embarrassing questions to those who did know, and as they were pledged to silence, forcing them into deliberate lies. One day at breakfast in the large dining-hall he entered into a conversation with the manager, that softly-treading little man in the French frock coat who was moving amiably and solicitously about among the diners and had stopped at Aschenbach's table for a few passing words. Just why, the guest asked negligently and casually, had disinfectants become so prevalent in Venice recently? "It has to do," was the evasive answer, "with a police regulation, and is intended to prevent any inconveniences or disturbances to the public health which might result from the exceptionally warm and threatening weather." . . . "The police are to be congratulated," Aschenbach answered; and after the exchange of a few remarks on the weather, the manager left.

Yet that same day, in the evening, after dinner, it happened that a little band of strolling singers from the city gave a performance in the front garden of the hotel. Two men and two women, they stood by the iron post of an arc-lamp and turned their whitened faces up towards the large terrace where the guests were enjoying this folk-recital over their coffee and cooling drinks. The hotel personnel, bell boys, waiters, and clerks from the office, could be seen listening by the doors of the vestibule. The Russian family, eager and precise in their amusements, had had wicker chairs placed in the garden in order to be nearer the performers; and they were sitting here in an appreciative semi-circle. Behind the ladies and gentlemen, in her turban-like kerchief, stood the old slave.

Mandolin, guitar, harmonica, and a squeaky violin were responding to the touch of the virtuoso beggars. Instrumental numbers alternated with songs, as when the younger of the women, with a sharp trembling voice, joined with the sweetly falsetto tenor in a languishing love duet. But the real talent and leader of the group was undoubtedly the other of the two men, the one with the guitar. He was a kind of *buffo* baritone, with not much of a voice, although he did have a gift for pantomime, and a remarkable comic energy. Often, with his large instrument under his arm, he would leave the rest of the group and, still acting, would intrude on the platform, where his antics were rewarded with encouraging laughter. Especially the Russians in their seats down front seemed to be enchanted with so much southern mobility, and their applause incited him to let himself out more and more boldly and assertively.

Aschenbach sat on the balustrade, cooling his lips now and then with a mixture of pomegranate juice and soda which glowed ruby red in his glass in front of him. His nerves took in the miserable notes, the vulgar crooning melodies; for passion lames the sense of discrimination, and surrenders in all seriousness to appeals which, in sober moments, are either humorously allowed for or rejected with annoyance. At the clown's antics his features bad twisted into a set painful smile. He sat there relaxed, although inwardly he was intensely awake; for six paces from him Tadzio was leaning against the stone hand-rail.

In the white belted coat which he often wore at meal times, he was standing in a position of spontaneous and inborn gracefulness, his left forearm on the railing, feet crossed, the right hand on a supporting hip; and he looked down at the street-singers with an expression which was hardly a smile, but only an aloof curiosity, a polite amiability. Often he would stand erect and, expanding his chest, would draw the white smock down under his leather belt with a beautiful gesture. And then too, the aging man observed with a tumult of fright and triumph how he would often turn his head over the left shoulder in the direction of his admirer, carefully and hesitatingly, or even with abruptness as though to attack by surprise. He did not meet Aschenbach's eyes, for a mean precaution compelled the transgressor to keep from staring at him: in the background of the terrace the women who guarded Tadzio were sitting, and things had reached a point where the lover had to fear that he might be noticed and suspected. Yes, he had often observed with a kind of numbness how, when Tadzio was near him, on the beach, in the hotel lobby, in the Piazza San Marco, they called him back, they were set on keeping him at a distance—and this wounded him frightfully, causing his pride unknown tortures which his conscience would not permit him to evade.

Meanwhile the guitar-player had begun a solo to his own accompaniment, a street-ballad popular throughout Italy. It had several strophes, and the entire company joined each time in the refrain, all singing and playing, while he managed to give a plastic and dramatic twist to the performance. Of slight build, with thin and impoverished features, he stood on the gravel, apart from his companions, in an attitude of insolent bravado, his shabby felt hat on the back of his head so that a bunch of his red hair jutted out from under the brim. And to the thrumming of the strings he flung his jokes up at the terrace in a penetrating recitative; while the veins were swelling on his forehead from the exertion of his performance. He did not seem of Venetian stock, but rather of the race of Neapolitan comedians, half pimp, half entertainer, brutal and audacious, dangerous and amusing. His song was stupid enough so far as the words went; but in his mouth, by his gestures, the movements of his body, his way of blinking significantly and letting the tongue play across his lips, it acquired something ambiguous, something vaguely repulsive. In addition to the customary civilian dress, he was wearing a sport shirt; and his skinny neck protruded above the soft collar, baring a noticeably large and active Adam's-apple. He was pale and snub-nosed. It was hard to fix an age to his beardless features, which seemed furrowed with grimaces and depravity; and the two wrinkles standing arrogantly, harshly, almost savagely between his reddish eyebrows were strangely suited to the smirk on his mobile lips. Yet what really prompted the lonely man to pay him keen attention was the observation that the questionable figure seemed also to provide its own questionable atmosphere. For each time they came to the refrain the singer, amid buffoonery and familiar handshakes, began a grotesque circular march which brought him immediately beneath Aschenbach's place; and each time this happened there blew up to the terrace from his clothes and body a strong carbolic smell.

After the song was ended, he began collecting money. He started with the Russians, who were evidently willing to spend, and then came up the stairs. Up here he showed himself just as humble as he had been bold during the performance. Cringing and bowing, he stole about among the tables, and a smile of obsequious cunning exposed his strong teeth, while the two wrinkles still stood ominously between his red eyebrows. This singular character collecting money to live on—they eyed him with a curiosity and a kind of repugnance, they tossed coins into his felt hat with the tips of their fingers, and were careful not to touch him. The elimination of the physical distance between the comedian and the audience, no matter how great the enjoyment may have been, always causes a certain uneasiness. He felt it, and tried to excuse it by grovelling. He came up to Aschenbach, and along with him the smell, which no one else seemed concerned about.

"Listen!" the recluse said in an undertone, almost mechanically. "They are disinfecting Venice. Why?" The jester answered hoarsely, "On account of the police. That is a precaution, sir, with such heat, and the sirocco. The sirocco is oppressive. It is not good for the health." He spoke as though astonished that any one could ask such things, and demonstrated with his open hand how oppressive the sirocco was. "Then there is no plague in Venice?" Aschenbach asked quietly, between his teeth. The clown's muscular features fell into a grimace of comical embarrassment. "A plague? What kind of plague? Perhaps our police are a plague? You like to joke! A plague! Of all things! A precautionary measure, you understand! A police regulation against the effects of the oppressive weather." He gesticulated. "Very well," Aschenbach said several times curtly and quietly; and he quickly dropped an unduly large coin into the hat. Then with his eyes he signalled the man to leave. He obeyed, smirking and bowing. But he had not reached the stairs before two hotel employees threw themselves upon him, and with their faces close to his began a whispered cross-examination. He shrugged his shoulders; he gave assurances, he swore that he had kept quiet—that was evident. He was released, and he returned to the garden; then after a short conference with his companions, he stepped out once more for a final song of thanks and leave-taking.

It was a rousing song which the recluse never recalled having heard before, a "big number" in incomprehensible dialect, with a laugh refrain in which the troupe joined regularly at the tops of their voices. At this point both the words and the accompaniment of the instruments stopped, with nothing left but a laugh which was somehow arranged rhythmically although very naturally done—and the soloist especially showed great talent in giving it a most deceptive vitality. At the renewal of his professional distance from the audience he had recovered all his boldness again, and the artificial laugh that he directed up towards the terrace was derisive. Even before the end of the articulate portion of the strophe, he seemed to struggle against an irresistible tickling. He gulped, his voice trembled, he pressed his hand over his mouth, he contorted his shoulders; and at the proper moment the ungovernable laugh broke out of him, burst into such real cackles that it was infectious and communicated itself to the audience, so that on the terrace also an unfounded hilarity, living off itself alone, started up. But this seemed to double the singer's exuberance. He bent his knees, he slapped his thighs, he nearly split himself; he no longer laughed, he shrieked. He pointed up with his finger, as though nothing were more comic than the laughing guests there, and finally everyone in the garden and on the verandah was laughing, even to the waiters, bell boys, and house-servants in the doorways.

Aschenbach was no longer resting in his chair; he sat upright, as if attempting to defend himself, or to escape. But the laughter, the whiffs of the hospital smell, and the boy's nearness combined to put him into a trance that held his mind and his senses hopelessly captive. In the general movement and distraction he ventured to glance across at Tadzio, and as he did so he dared observe that the boy, in reply to his glance, was equally serious, much as though he had modelled his conduct and expression after those of one man, and the prevalent mood had no effect on him since this one man was not part of it. This portentous childish obedience had something so disarming and overpowering about it that the grey-haired man could hardly restrain himself from burying his face in his hands. It had also seemed to him that Tadzio's occasional stretching and quick breathing indicated a complaint, a congestion, of the lungs. "He is sickly, he will probably not grow old," he thought repeatedly with that positiveness which is often a peculiar relief to desire and passion. And along with pure solitude he had a feeling of rakish gratification.

Meanwhile the Venetians had ended and were leaving. Applause accompanied them, and their leader did not miss the opportunity to cover his retreat with further jests. His bows, the kisses he blew, were laughed at—and so he doubled them. When his companions were already gone, he acted as though he had hurt himself by backing into a lamp-post, and he crept through the gate seemingly crippled with pain. Then he suddenly threw off the mask of comic hard luck, stood upright, hurried away jauntily, stuck out his tongue insolently at the guests on the terrace, and slipped into the darkness. The company was breaking up; Tadzio had been missing from the balustrade for some time. But, to the displeasure of the waiters, the lonely man sat for a long while over the remains of his pomegranate drink. Night advanced. Time was crumbling. In the house of his parents many years back there had been an hour glass—of a sudden he saw the fragile and expressive instrument again, as though it were standing in front of him. Fine and noiseless the rust-red sand was running through the glass neck; and since it was getting low in the upper half, a speedy little vortex had been formed there.

As early as the following day, in the afternoon, he had made new progress in his obstinate baiting of the people he met—and this time he had all possible success. He walked from the Piazza of St. Mark's into the English travelling bureau located there; and after changing some money at the cash desk, he put on the expression of a distrustful foreigner and launched his fatal question at the attendant clerk. He was a Britisher; he wore a woollen suit, and was still young, with close-set eyes, and had that characteristic stolid reliability which is so peculiarly and strikingly appealing in the tricky, nimble-witted South. He began, "No reason for alarm, sir. A regulation without any serious significance. Such measures are often taken to anticipate the unhealthy effects of the heat and the sirocco . . ." But as he raised his blue eyes, he met the stare of the foreigner, a tired and somewhat unhappy stare focussed on his lips with a touch of scorn. Then the Englishman blushed. "At least," he continued in an emotional undertone, "that is the official explanation which people here are content to accept. I will admit that there is something more behind it." And then in his frank and leisurely manner he told the truth.

For several years now Indian cholera had shown a heightened tendency to spread and migrate. Hatched in the warm swamps of the Ganges delta, rising with the noxious breath of that luxuriant, unfit primitive world and island wilderness which is shunned by humans and where the tiger crouches in the bamboo thickets, the plague had raged continuously and with unusual strength in Hindustan, had reached eastwards to China, westwards to Afghanistan and Persia, and following the chief caravan routes, had carried its terrors to Astrachan, and even to Moscow. But while Europe was trembling lest the spectre continue its advance from there across the country, it had been transported over the sea by Syrian merchantmen, and had turned up almost simultaneously in several Mediterranean ports, had raised its head in Toulon and Malaga, had showed its mask several times in Palermo and Naples, and seemed permanently entrenched through Calabria and Apulia. The north of the peninsula had been spared. Yet in the middle of this May in Venice the frightful vibrions were found on one and the same day in the blackish wasted bodies of a cabin boy and a woman who sold greengroceries. The cases were kept secret. But within a week there were ten, twenty, thirty more, and in various sections. A man from the Austrian provinces who had made a pleasure trip to Venice for a few days, returned to his home town and died with unmistakable symptoms—and that is how the first reports of the pestilence in the lagoon city got into the German newspapers. The Venetian authorities answered that the city's health conditions had never been better, and took the most necessary preventive measures. But probably the food supply had been infected. Denied and glossed over, death was eating its way along the narrow streets, and its dissemination was especially favoured by the premature summer heat which made the water of the canals lukewarm. Yes, it seemed as though the plague had got renewed strength, as though the tenacity and fruitfulness of its stimuli had doubled. Cases of recovery were rare. Out of a hundred attacks, eighty were fatal, and in the most horrible manner. For the plague moved with utter savagery, and often showed that most dangerous form, which is called "the drying." Water from the blood vessels collected in pockets, and the blood was unable to carry this off. Within a few hours the victim was parched, his blood became as thick as glue, and he stifled amid cramps and hoarse groans. Lucky for him if, as sometimes happened, the attack took the form of a light discomfiture followed by a profound coma from which he seldom or never awakened. At the beginning of June the pesthouse of the Ospedale Civico had quietly filled; there was not much room left in the two orphan asylums, and a frightfully active commerce was kept up between the wharf of the Fondamenta Nuove and San Michele, the burial island. But there was the fear of a general drop in prosperity. The recently opened art exhibit in the public gardens was to be considered, along with the heavy losses which in case of panic or unfavourable rumours, would threaten business, the hotels, the entire elaborate system for exploiting foreigners—and as these considerations evidently carried more weight than love of truth or respect for international agreements, the city authorities upheld obstinately their policy of silence and denial. The chief health officer had resigned from his post in indignation, and been promptly replaced by a more tractable personality. The people knew this; and the corruption of their superiors, together with the predominating insecurity, the exceptional condition into which the prevalence of death had plunged the city, induced a certain demoralization of the lower classes, encouraging shady and anti-social impulses which manifested themselves in licence, profligacy, and a rising crime wave. Contrary to custom, many drunkards were seen in the evenings; it was said that at night nasty mobs made the streets unsafe. Burglaries and even murders became frequent, for it had already been proved on two occasions that persons who had presumably fallen victim to the plague had in reality been dispatched with poison by their own relatives. And professional debauchery assumed abnormal and obtrusive proportions such as had never been known here before, and to an extent which is usually found only in the southern parts of the country and in the Orient.

The Englishman pronounced the final verdict on these facts. "You would do well," he concluded, "to leave to-day rather than to-morrow. It cannot be much more than a couple of days before a quarantine zone is declared." "Thank you," Aschenbach said, and left the office.

The square lay sunless and stifling. Unsuspecting foreigners sat in front of the cafés, or stood among the pigeons in front of the church and watched the swarms of birds flapping their wings, crowding one another, and pecking at grains of corn offered them in open palms. The recluse was feverishly excited, triumphant in his possession of the truth. But it had left him with a bad taste in his mouth, and a weird horror in his heart. As he walked up and down the flagstones of the gorgeous court he was weighing an action which would meet the situation and would absolve him. This evening after dinner he could approach the woman with the pearls and make her a speech; he had figured it out word for word: "Permit a foreigner, madam, to give you some useful advice, a warning, which is being withheld from you through self-interest. Leave immediately with Tadzio and your daughters! Venice is full of the plague." Then he could lay a farewell hand on the head of this tool of a mocking divinity, turn away, and flee this morass. But he felt at the same time that he was very far from seriously desiring such a move. He would retract it, would disengage himself from it. . . . But when we are distracted we loathe most the thought of retracing our steps. He recalled a white building, ornamented with inscriptions which glistened in the evening and in whose transparent mysticism his mind's eye had lost itself—and then that strange wanderer's form which had awakened in the aging man the roving hankerings of youth after the foreign and the remote. And the thought of return, the thought of prudence and soberness, effort, mastery, disgusted him to such an extent that his face was distorted with an expression of physical nausea. "It must be kept silent!" he whispered heavily. And: "I will keep silent!" The consciousness of his share in the facts and the guilt intoxicated him, much as a little wine intoxicates a tired brain. The picture of the diseased and neglected city hovering desolately before him aroused vague hopes beyond the bounds of reason, but with an egregious sweetness. What was the scant happiness he had dreamed of a moment ago, compared with these expectations? What were art and virtue worth to him, over against the advantages of chaos? He kept silent, and remained in Venice.

This same night he had a frightful dream, if one can designate as a dream a bodily and mental experience which occurred to him in the deepest sleep, completely independent of him, and with a physical realness, although he never saw himself present or moving about among the incidents; but their stage rather was his soul itself, and they broke in from without, trampling down his resistance—a profound and spiritual resistance—by sheer force; and when they had passed through, they left his substance, the culture of his lifetime, crushed and annihilated behind them.

It began with anguish, anguish and desire, and a frightened curiosity as to what was coming. It was night, and his senses were on the watch. From far off a grumble, an uproar, was approaching, a jumble of noises. Clanking, blaring, and dull thunder, with shrill shouts and a definite whine in a long drawn out u-sound—all this was sweetly, ominously interspersed and dominated by the deep cooing of wickedly persistent flutes which charmed the bowels in a shamelessly penetrative manner. But he knew one word; it was veiled, and yet would name what was approaching: "The foreign god!" Vaporous fire began to glow; then he recognized mountains like those about his summer house. And in the scattered light, from high up in the woods, among tree trunks and crumbling moss-grown rocks—people, beasts, a throng, a raging mob plunged twisting and whirling downwards, and made the hill swarm with bodies, flames, tumult, and a riotous round dance. Women, tripped by over-long fur draperies which hung from their waists, were holding up tambourines and beating on them, their groaning heads flung back. Others swung sparking firebrands and bare daggers, or wore hissing snakes about the middle of their bodies, or shrieking held their breasts in their two hands. Men with horns on their foreheads, shaggy-haired, girded with hides, bent back their necks and raised their arms and thighs, clashed brass cymbals and beat furiously at kettledrums, while smooth boys prodded he-goats with wreathed sticks, climbing on their horns and falling off with shouts when they bounded. And the bacchantes wailed the word with the soft consonants and the drawn out u-sound, at once sweet and savage, like nothing ever heard before. In one place it rang out as though piped into the air by stags, and it was echoed in another by many voices, in wild triumph—with it they incited one another to dance and to fling out their arms and legs, and it was never silent. But everything was pierced and dominated by the deep coaxing flute. He who was fighting against this experience—did it not coax him too with its shameless penetration, into the feast and the excesses of the extreme sacrifice? His repugnance, his fear, were keen—he was honourably set on defending himself to the very last against the barbarian, the foe to intellectual poise and dignity. But the noise, the howling, multiplied by the resonant walls of the hills, grew, took the upper hand, swelled to a fury of rapture. Odours oppressed the senses, the pungent smell of the bucks, the scent of moist bodies, and a waft of stagnant water, with another smell, something familiar, the smell of wounds and prevalent disease. At the beating of the drum his heart fluttered, his head was spinning, he was caught in a frenzy, in a blinding deafening lewdness—and he yearned to join the ranks of the god. The obscene symbol, huge, wooden, was uncovered and raised up; then they howled the magic word with more abandon. Foaming at the mouth, they raged, teased one another with ruttish gestures and caressing hands; laughing and groaning, they stuck the goads into one another's flesh and licked the blood from their limbs. But the dreamer now was with them, in them, and he belonged to the foreign god. Yes, they were he himself, as they hurled themselves biting and tearing upon the animals, got entangled in steaming rags, and fell in promiscuous unions on the torn moss, in sacrifice to their god. And his soul tasted the unchastity and fury of decay.

When he awakened from the affliction of this dream he was unnerved, shattered, and hopelessly under the power of the demon. He no longer avoided the inquisitive glances of other people; he did not care if he was exciting their suspicions. And as a matter of fact they were fleeing, travelling elsewhere. Numerous bathing houses stood empty, the occupants of the dining-hall became more and more scattered, and in the city now one rarely saw a foreigner. The truth seemed to have leaked out; the panic, despite the reticence of those whose interests were involved, seemed no longer avoidable. But the woman with the pearls remained with her family, either because the rumours had not yet reached her, or because she was too proud and fearless to heed them. Tadzio remained. And to Aschenbach, in his infatuation, it seemed at times as though flight and death might remove all the disturbing elements of life around them, and he stay here alone with the boy. Yes, by the sea in the forenoon when his eyes rested heavily, irresponsibly, unwaveringly on the thing he coveted, or when, as the day was ending, he followed shamelessly after him through streets where the hideous death lurked in secret—at such times the atrocious seemed to him rich in possibilities, and laws of morality had dropped away.

Like any lover, he wanted to please; and he felt a bitter anguish lest it might not be possible. He added bright youthful details to his dress, he put on jewels, and used perfumes. During the day he often spent much time over his toilet, and came to the table strikingly dressed, excited, and in suspense. In the light of the sweet youthfulness which had done this to him, he detested his aging body. The sight of his grey hair, his sharp features, plunged him into shame and hopelessness. It induced him to attempt rejuvenating his body and appearance. He often visited the hotel barber.

Beneath the barber's apron, leaning back in the chair under the gossiper's expert hands, he winced to observe his reflection in the mirror.

"Grey," he said, making a wry face.

"A little," the man answered. "Due entirely to a slight neglect, an indifference to outward things, which is conceivable in people of importance, but it is not exactly praiseworthy. And all the less so since such persons are above prejudice in matters of nature or art. If the moral objections of certain people to the art of cosmetics were to be logically extended to the care of the teeth, they would give no slight offence. And after all, we are just as old as we feel, and under some circumstances grey hair would actually stand for more of an untruth than the despised correction. In your case, sir, you are entitled to the natural colour of your hair. Will you permit me simply to return what belongs to you?"

"How is that?" Aschenbach asked.

Then the orator washed his client's hair with two kinds of water, one clear and one dark, and it was as black as in youth. Following this, he curled it with irons into soft waves, stepped back, and eyed his work.

"All that is left now," he said, "would be to freshen up the skin a little."

And like someone who cannot finish, cannot satisfy himself, he passed with quickening energy from one manipulation to another. Aschenbach rested comfortably, incapable of resistance, or rather his hopes aroused by what was taking place. In the glass he saw his brows arch more evenly and decisively. His eyes became longer; their brilliance was heightened by a light touching-up of the lids. A little lower, where the skin had been a leatherish brown, he saw a delicate crimson tint grow beneath a deft application of colour. His lips, bloodless a little while past, became full, and as red as raspberries. The furrows in the cheeks and about the mouth, the wrinkles of the eyes, disappeared beneath lotions and cream. With a knocking heart he beheld a blossoming youth. Finally the beauty specialist declared himself content, after the manner of such people, by obsequiously thanking the man he had been serving. "A trifling assistance," he said, as he applied one parting touch. "Now the gentleman can fall in love unhesitatingly." He walked away, fascinated; he was happy as in a dream, timid and bewildered. His necktie was red, his broad-brimmed straw hat was trimmed with a variegated band.

A tepid storm wind had risen. It was raining sparsely and at intervals, but the air was damp, thick, and filled with the smell of things rotting. All around him he heard a fluttering, pattering, and swishing; and under the fever of his cosmetics it seemed to him as though evil wind-spirits were haunting the place, impure sea birds which rooted and gnawed at the food of the condemned and befouled it with their droppings. For the sultriness destroyed his appetite, and the fancy suggested itself that the foods were poisoned with contaminating substances. Tracking the boy one afternoon, Aschenbach had plunged deep into the tangled centre of the diseased city. He was becoming uncertain of where he was, since the alleys, waterways, bridges, and little squares of the labyrinth were all so much alike, and he was no longer even sure of directions. He was absorbed with the problem of keeping the pursued figure in sight. And, driven to disgraceful subterfuges, flattening himself against walls, hiding behind the backs of other people, for a long time he did not notice the weariness, the exhaustion, with which emotion and the continual suspense had taxed his mind and his body. Tadzio walked behind his companions. He always allowed the governess and the nunlike sisters to precede him in the narrow places; and loitering behind alone, he would turn his head occasionally to look over his shoulder and make sure by a glance of his peculiarly dark-grey eyes that his admirer was following. He saw him, and did not betray him. Drunk with the knowledge of this, lured forward by those eyes, led meekly by his passion, the lover stole after his unseemly hope—but finally he was cheated and lost sight of him. The Poles had crossed a short arching bridge; the height of the curve hid them from the pursuer, and when he himself had arrived there he no longer saw them. He hunted for them vainly in three directions, straight ahead and to either side along the narrow dirty wharf. In the end he was so tired and unnerved that he had to give up the search.

His head was on fire, his body was covered with a sticky sweat, his knees trembled. He could no longer endure the thirst that was torturing him, and he looked around for some immediate relief. From a little vegetable store he bought some fruit—strawberries, soft and overly ripe—and he ate them as he walked. A very charming, forsaken little square opened up before him. He recognized it; here he had made his frustrated plans for flight weeks ago. He let himself sink down on the steps of the cistern in the middle of the square, and laid his head against the stone cylinder. It was quiet; grass was growing up through the pavement; refuse was scattered about. Among the weather-beaten, unusually tall houses surrounding him there was one like a palace, with little lion-covered balconies, and Gothic windows with blank emptiness behind them. On the ground floor of another house was a drug store. Warm gusts of wind occasionally carried the smell of carbolic acid.

He sat there, he, the master, the artist of dignity, the author of The Wretch, a work which had, in such accurate symbols, renounced vagabondage and the depths of misery, had denied all sympathy with the engulfed, and had cast out the outcast; the man who had arrived and, victor over his own knowledge, had outgrown all irony and acclimatized himself to the obligations of public confidence; whose reputation was official, whose name had been knighted, and on whose style boys were urged to pattern themselves—he sat there. His eyelids were shut; only now and then a mocking uneasy side-glance slipped out from beneath them. And his loose lips, set off by the cosmetics, formed isolated words of the strange dream-logic created by his half-slumbering brain.

"For beauty, Phaedrus, mark me, beauty alone is both divine and visible at once; and thus it is the road of the sensuous; it is, little Phaedrus, the road of the artist to the spiritual. But do you now believe, my dear, that they can ever attain wisdom and true human dignity for whom the road to the spiritual leads through the senses? Or do you believe rather (I leave the choice to you) that this is a pleasant but perilous road, a really wrong and sinful road, which necessarily leads astray? For you must know that we poets cannot take the road of beauty without having Eros join us and set himself up as our leader. Indeed, we may even be heroes after our fashion, and hardened warriors, though we be like women, for passion is our exaltation, and our desire must remain love—that is our pleasure and our disgrace. You now see, do you not, that we poets cannot be wise and dignified? That we necessarily go astray, necessarily remain lascivious, and adventurers in emotion? The mastery of our style is all lies and foolishness, our renown and honour are a farce, the confidence of the masses in us is highly ridiculous, and the training of the public and of youth through art is a precarious undertaking which should be forbidden. For how indeed could he be a fit instructor who is born with a natural leaning towards the precipice? We might well disavow it and reach after dignity, but wherever we turn it attracts us. Let us, say, renounce the dissolvent of knowledge, since knowledge, Phaedrus, has no dignity or strength. It is aware, it understands and pardons, but without reserve and form. It feels sympathy with the precipice, it is the precipice. This then we abandon with firmness, and from now on our efforts matter only by their yield of beauty, or in other words, simplicity, greatness, and new rigour, form, and a second type of openness. But form and openness, Phaedrus, lead to intoxication and to desire, lead the noble perhaps into sinister revels of emotion which his own beautiful rigour rejects as infamous, lead to the precipice, yes they too lead to the precipice. They lead us poets there, I say, since we cannot force ourselves, since we can merely let ourselves out And now I am going, Phaedrus. You stay here; and when you no longer see me, then you go too."

A few days later, as Gustav von Aschenbach was not feeling well, he left the beach hotel at a later hour in the morning than usual. He had to fight against certain attacks of vertigo which were only partially physical and were accompanied by a pronounced malaise, a feeling of bafflement and hopelessness—while he was not certain whether this had to do with conditions outside him or with his own nature. In the lobby he noticed a large pile of luggage ready for shipment; he asked the door-keeper who it was that was leaving, and heard in answer the Polish title which he had learned secretly. He accepted this without any alteration of his sunken features, with that curt elevation of the head by which one acknowledges something he does not need to know. Then he asked, "When?" The answer was, "After lunch." He nodded, and went to the beach.

It was not very inviting. Rippling patches of rain retreated across the wide flat water separating the beach from the first long sand-bank. An air of autumn, of things past their prime, seemed to lie over the pleasure spot which had once been so alive with colour and was now almost abandoned. The sand was no longer kept clean. A camera, seemingly without an owner, stood on its tripod by the edge of the sea; and a black cloth thrown over it was flapping noisily in the wind.

Tadzio, with the three or four companions still left, was moving about to the right in front of his family's cabin. And midway between the sea and the row of bathing houses, lying back in his chair with a robe over his knees, Aschenbach looked at him once more. The game, which was not being supervised since the women were probably occupied with preparations for the journey, seemed to have no rules, and it was degenerating. The stocky boy with the sleek black hair who was called Jaschu had been angered and blinded by sand flung in his face. He forced Tadzio into a wrestling match which quickly ended in the fall of the beauty, who was weaker. But as though in the hour of parting the servile feelings of the inferior had turned to merciless brutality and were trying to get vengeance for a long period of slavery, the victor did not let go of the boy underneath, but knelt on his back and pressed his face so persistently into the sand that Tadzio, already breathless from the struggle, was in danger of strangling. His attempts to shake off the weight were fitful; for moments they stopped entirely and were resumed again as mere twitchings. Enraged, Aschenbach was about to spring to the rescue, when the torturer finally released his victim. Tadzio, very pale, raised himself halfway and sat motionless for several minutes, resting on one arm, with rumpled hair and glowering eyes. Then he stood up completely, and moved slowly away. They called him, cheerfully at first, then anxiously and imploringly; he did not listen. The swarthy boy, who seemed to regret his excesses immediately afterwards, caught up with him and tried to placate him. A movement of the shoulder put him at his distance. Tadzio went down obliquely to the water. He was barefoot, and wore his striped linen suit with the red bow.

He lingered on the edge of the water with his head down, drawing figures in the wet sand with one toe; then he went into the shallows, which did not cover his knees in the deepest place, crossed them leisurely, and arrived at the sand-bank. He stood there a moment, his face turned to the open sea;

soon after, he began stepping slowly to the left along the narrow stretch of exposed ground. Separated from the mainland by the expanse of water, separated from his companions by a proud moodiness, he moved along, a strongly isolated and unrelated figure with fluttering hair—placed out there in the sea, the wind, against the vague mists. He stopped once more to look around. And suddenly, as though at some recollection, some impulse, with one hand on his hip he turned the upper part of his body in a beautiful twist which began from the base—and he looked over his shoulder towards the shore. The watcher sat there, as he had sat once before when for the first time these twilight-grey eyes had turned at the doorway and met his own. His head, against the back of the chair, had slowly followed the movements of the boy walking yonder. Now, simultaneously with this glance it rose and sank on his breast, so that his eyes looked out from underneath, while his face took on the loose, inwardly relaxed expression of deep sleep. But it seemed to him as though the pale and lovely lure out there were smiling to him, nodding to him; as though, removing his hand from his hip, he were signalling to come out, were vaguely guiding towards egregious promises. And, as often before, he stood up to follow him.

Some minutes passed before any one hurried to the aid of the man who had collapsed into one corner of his chair. He was brought to his room. And on the same day a respectfully shocked world received the news of his death.

THE END

www.ingramcontent.com/pod-product-compliance
Ingram Content Group UK Ltd.
Pitfield, Milton Keynes, MK11 3LW, UK
UKHW011341060725
6747UKWH00025B/374